THE ABDUCTION PROJECT

The Abduction Project

ERMA JONES

Copyright © 2024 **Star Light Publishing**

All rights reserved. No part of this publication may be reproduced, distributed, or transmitted in any form or by any means, including photocopying, recording, or other electronic or mechanical methods, without the prior written permission of the publisher, except in the case of brief quotations embodied in critical reviews and certain other noncommercial uses permitted by copyright law. For permission requests, write to the publisher, addressed "Attention: Book Rights and Permission," at the address below.

Published in the United States of America

ISBN 978-1-961507-63-0 (SC)
ISBN 978-1-961507-61-6 (HC)
ISBN 978-1-961507-62-3 (Ebook)

Star Light Publishing
222 West 6th Street
Suite 400, San Pedro, CA, 90731
ermajones23@yahoo.com

Order Information and Rights Permission:

Quantity sales. Special discounts might be available on quantity purchases by corporations, associations, and others. For details, contact the publisher at the address above.

For Book Rights Adaptation and other Rights Permission. Call us at toll-free 1-888-945-8513 or send us an email at admin@stellarliterary.com.

CHAPTER 1

The envelope was sitting on the table in the dining room, resting against the napkin holder and pepper shaker. The lights in the old split-level ranch-style house was a dingy yellow dim light that filled the room. So, Amanda didn't see the envelope the first time she walked past the table. It had rained all day that day, and the old house was damp and cool even though it was in the middle of May. Amanda walked into the living room and turned the thermostat up.

She walked back into the dining room and there it was, a long white envelope that read "Harvard." Amanda's heart jolted and her palms began to sweat as she grabbed the envelope off the table, knocking the pepper shaker to its side. Her heart erupted as she read over the letter for the first time. She couldn't lose the smile that expanded across her face. Her hands trembled as she read her acceptance letter one last time.

"Harvard! Grandma, your baby is going to Harvard!" she screamed.

She swung around and looked at her grandmother who was sitting in her recliner in front of the TV. She was a petite old dark-skinned woman with long gray hair. She wore a pink housecoat with blue flowers on the collar and pink house slippers. She smiled at Amanda.

"Your hard work paid off. Who said an inner-city kid from Collins High school can't go to Harvard?" Amanda's grandmother said.

"My letter said the scholarship pays for everything. I don't have to worry about a thing," Amanda said as she pressed the letter to her chest.

"I thought being valedictorian was something, but this, this, I can't put into words."

"Amanda, you are smart. Your grandfather told you before he died you could do whatever you want to do, and he would have been proud of you."

"If he was here."

"I know I'm proud of you, because I know you could leave Chicago and never look back. Take your brother and go to Boston and never look back."

"You are going too, grandma. I can't leave home without you."

"Don't worry about me, child. I'll be all right, Joe and I."

Amanda looked over in the corner of the living room by the front door at Joe, her grandmother's Golden Retriever lying on a rug. He had grown old, gained a little weight, and became lazy. He raised his head and barked when Amanda's grandma mentioned his name.

"Tell her we'll be all right, Joe. Joe would keep me company."

"But who will go to the store for you and remind you of your medicine?" Amanda asked.

"I could do those things for myself. Don't worry about me."

"It's time you start thinking of yourself. You can't take care of everybody."

"But you are not everybody, you are my grandma," Amanda said as a wave moved through her stomach. She wanted to go to Boston and attend Harvard, but she didn't want to leave her grandma in Chicago on the west side of town, where there was more gang violence than in Afghanistan. For as long as she could remember, she wanted to go to Harvard. She remembered working a double shift at McDonald's so she could afford to pay for her tutoring for the SATs where she got a high score and a perfect score on the Math portion of the test.

Math always came easy for Amanda, and she excelled in Science too. Her guidance counselor told her the sky was the limit, and the Admissions Counselor for Harvard was impressed she had the right amount of extracurricular activities. She was a Girl Scout, she was in the honor society, and she was class president. Between her grades and her scores on the SATs, she was a shoo-in for Harvard.

She looked at her letter one last time before sticking it back in the envelope.

"I better get dinner ready," she said as she walked into the galley style kitchen. It was a small kitchen with cabinets along the wall. It had a long counter extending from one side of the kitchen to the other, and a refrigerator and stove on the opposite side of the counter.

Amanda took out some pork chops that had thawed in the refrigerator and prepared them for broiling. She steamed some green beans and made a pan of cornbread. Her grandma loved her cornbread. It was soft and flaky with a hint of sweetness. She remembered when she first learned to make cornbread. Her grandmother showed her how to measure the cornmeal and put in the right amount of flour. Now she is an expert. She loved her grandparents. They took her in when she was ten, together with her brother Steve who was only five. She never knew her father and her mother were in and out of jail. The Department of Children and Family Services had taken them from their mother because of their mother's drug problem. They placed the children with their grandparents who were proud to take them in.

"Steve! Dinner!" Amanda called.

Steve, a tall skinny kid of thirteen, wearing a Bulls jersey and jeans, ran downstairs. He threw his math book on the table.

"Could you help me with my math after dinner?" he asked Amanda.

"Yes, but first get your book off the table and sit down."

Her grandmother got up and slowly walked into the dining room. She sat down and they ate. A police squad car with flashing lights and sirens drove past the house.

"I can't wait to go to Boston," Steve said.

"It would be nice to get away from all of the crimes," Amanda replied.

"Amanda, you have a great opportunity, even more than what your mother had. Use it and go far."

"I will grandma," Amanda replied.

"I am going to go to college too grandma. I don't know about Harvard, but you will be proud of me too," Steve added.

"I know I will Steve."

"Grandma, I wish you would change your mind and go with us," Amanda persuaded.

"I can't leave my house. I have too much invested in this old thing."

"I could buy you a new one."

"Child, you have to finish college first and by that time you will be thinking about getting married. You will forget about poor old me."

Amanda thought about what her grandma had said. She could never forget her grandma, not after all the sacrifice her grandmother had gone through to keep her and Steve together. Her grandmother and grandfather worked double shifts as housemaids at the Drake Hotel to keep food on the table and put clothes on their backs.

Once when their lights got cut off, their grandmother stood in line at the light company for four hours just to get an extension on the light bill. Her grandmother went through a lot for her and Steve. No, she couldn't just forget her.

"I won't forget you grandma. I'll call you every day."

"I'll call you too, Granny," Steve said smiling, as he swallowed the rest of his pork chop.

"I know you will Steve," his grandmother said, amazed at how much Steve could eat. He was a skinny kid, but he had grown as tall as his grandfather. They finished dinner and Steve ran back upstairs. Amanda's grandmother got up from the table.

"You want me to help you with the dishes?" she asked as she picked up her plate from the table.

"No Granny, you sit down. I'll get the dishes," Amanda said. She took the leftover food, placed them in storage bowls and put them in the refrigerator.

"Amanda, you work too hard," her grandmother said as she walked into the living room.

"I don't mind, Granny," Amanda said as she watched her grandmother walk slowly to her recliner, showing signs of the hard work she did over the years for her and Steve. That hard work put her grandfather in his grave, Amanda thought as she walked back into the kitchen. Doing the dishes was just a little token of her appreciation. Now, all she has to do is convince her grandmother to go to Boston with her and Steve. And that wasn't going to be easy, because her grandmother could be stubborn, but she could be stubborn too. She was not going to give up without a fight.

She dried the dishes and placed them in the cabinet, walked out of the kitchen, and turned off the light. She checked Joe's water bowl to see if he had enough water. Then she went into the living room and sat on the couch. Her grandmother was unwinding some yarn for crocheting. Amanda looked at her grandmother's trembling bony fingers slowly unwrapping the yarn, her eyes squinting through her drug store reading glasses as she patted her feet on the shaggy old green carpet and hummed old church spirituals. Amanda picked up the remote. She turned the TV to HBO.

"No, I won't leave her. Not without a fight. And a fight is probably what I will get," she thought as she watched her grandmother.

A hundred miles north of Chicago, in the woods concealed behind some trees was a US Military unit, which had set up camp and was monitoring the African-American community. Lieutenant Aiden Baxter of the planet Malatha, an earthlike planet in the Gamma Quadrant of space, was looking over the massive list of names that Colonel Jackson of the US Marines gave him. Col. Jackson was a tall and muscular white man who served in the military for twenty years. Now he was forty and had traveled all over the world.

"These are all the African-American women from infant to sixty in this region," he said, feeling a little uneasy.

Ever since the US government made contact with the Malatha alien race, he had to meet with them and negotiate with them. They weren't an angry race of men, but their demands were simple. They wanted all of the African-American women from infant to sixty. They didn't want the men. They only wanted women.

When the Secretary of State asked Colonel Bardolph Galveston, the alien in charge of the invasion, why they wanted women, he simply answered, "The Malatha government wants all of the African-American women from infant to sixty to be brides for our Malatha soldiers. They were once deployed in deep space where they were isolated from civilization for many years. They had grown in number, and now there is a shortage of women in Malatha for the soldiers because there was no female companionship for them on our planet. The soldiers had become wild and uncontrollable. The Malatha government thought of every solution available to try to control their soldiers, but every attempt failed. The only solution was to find companionship."

"The Malatha scientist searched the galaxy and came across Earth. Upon discovery, the African-American women have the same enzyme in their DNA as the Malatha soldiers. Because of that, they would be a perfect match. This DNA enzyme was developed in women at the time of slavery because the African-American women are the descendants of slaves. They had the enzyme needed by our soldiers," he added.

"We have the military ready. We are going to strike at nine o'clock," Col. Jackson said to Col. Galveston, a tall olive-skinned man with black straight hair and a beard. Col. Jackson was surprised he looked amazingly human. He wore a dark blue two-piece uniform with strange metals on the right side of his chest, a white belt which held what looked like a large jagged-edged knife and a phaser gun. He stood an inch taller than Col. Jackson, so he must have been about six feet five and inches tall, Col. Jackson thought.

Col. Galveston was also in the military for over twenty years. *Earth* years. Time for Malatha people was the same as Earth. They just lived a lot longer because they were more advanced in medicine and technology.

Galveston had seen about a third of the charted galaxy and he had also been in combat as well. He knew how to handle a developing planet like Earth and he was a man who got what he wanted. He sensed the fear in Jackson and that's how he wanted it.

"Good," he said to Col. Jackson.

"Aiden!" he called his lieutenant who was still looking over the list.

"Yes, sir," Aiden said as he saluted his colonel.

"Go and see if everything is ready. I want to be ready to depart before sunrise."

"Yes, sir," Aiden said as he saluted once more. He walked out of the tent and into the woods where there was a large oval-shaped metallic black ship nestled behind some trees. Aiden pressed his hand on a panel on the wall and a door rose up and he stepped inside. Once inside he looked around an enormous room large enough to hold twenty million people.

He walked around every department of the ship. It had a lounge, a dining hall, a café, a bar, a music lounge, a viewing area for entertainment, a dance hall, and a jail, just to name a few. The ship had everything a small city would have.

Aiden walked around once more before he called Col. Galveston to tell him everything was in order. He checked the restrooms and sleeping areas. He also checked on the other soldiers assigned to run all of those departments. Everything was in order. He raised his wrist to call his colonel when he thought about the medical tents.

He called his colonel and told him that the ship was in order and was ready to go. Galveston walked over to a large map on the screen in the tent where Col. Jackson was standing.

"Everything is ready."

His eyes sparkled and he clapped his hands to his chest.

"Are your men ready to strike?" he asked smiling.

"We are," Jackson said.

"We do this all the time. We could be in and out of the hot zone in about two hours. We will strike so fast they won't know what hit them. We have the best military in the world," he added.

"We don't want any casualties. We want the women untouched," Galveston said.

"We won't hurt them. We are working with tear gas and rubber bullets," Jackson replied.

"What about the men?" Galveston asked.

"We will handle them when all of this is over. Our first priority is the women," Col. Jackson said as he looked at the map.

Aiden left the ship and walked further into the woods where there was a makeshift medical tent set up for the women and people wearing biohazard suits.

"Is everything ready?" he asked Dr. Edger of Malatha.

"We are all set up to examine the women before they board the ship. We have everything in place if everything goes well. We should be through with our exams before sunrise."

"Good. Carry on," Aiden said.

He walked back to the tent where Galveston and Jackson were.

"Everything is in place."

"Good job. Aiden, you would make a good commanding officer one day," Galveston remarked.

"Well, it's time. I'm going to call my troops and begin the strike," Col. Jackson got on the radio and commanded the strike. The US Military pulled up in trucks in every African-American community in the US and began taking the women. They caught them off guard. They stormed in the houses and took them.

The people tried to fight back, but they were no match for the military. Some women tried to hide, but the soldiers had infrared heat sensors and found everyone. The men who tried to fight back were shot by the soldiers and left for dead.

The invasion went as planned and the soldiers had gathered all of the women and began their journey back to the camp. Some black men tried to follow the trucks but were cut off and stopped by other soldiers. The first of the trucks came in and Aiden stretched out his arms to help direct them to the camp. His eyes danced but he flinched hard to keep himself from smiling. Galveston looked at the truck and his heart overflowed as he tapped his feet. Aiden and his men directed the trucks to the medical tents where the women could be examined.

"All right, get the women off the truck in single files," Aiden said to the soldiers. The women exited the trucks and moved to the medical tents in single files.

"Look at them. They are beautiful," Galveston said.

Aiden looked and smiled. All of the women were a beautiful sight of ebony rose, like the picture of an Earth woman in the magazine that Aiden once saw. Now all of his dreams of one day having a family will come true.

"They are beautiful," he said to Galveston.

CHAPTER 2

Amanda was watching TV when she heard a loud noise outside her window. She looked outside and large green military trucks drove up and stopped in front of her house. Soldiers with machine guns jumped out and ran into the building across the street. Moments later, they came out dragging women and putting them in the trucks.

A riot broke out and people began to fight the soldiers. They ran and cried. The soldiers seized the men, but the ones who fought back were shot and left lying on the street. Two soldiers came to Amanda's house and Amanda's heart jumped to her throat. Her legs began to shake, and her eyes widened.

"Grandma!" she called. Her grandmother was asleep on her recliner when the soldiers pounded on the door.

"Granny!" Amanda called again.

Her grandma jumped up. Her heart raced and waves moved through her stomach. She got up and slowly went to the door. She opened the door slightly and peeked out.

"Yes," she said as US Marine Sgt. Lewis pushed open the door and stormed in. He was a tall medium-built man with short red hair and a goatee. His adrenaline was flowing and he had psyched himself up to show force.

He looked around and saw Amanda, rushed over and grabbed her by the arm.

"Are you Amanda?" he asked.

"Yes," Amanda forced out and felt like her throat had swollen shut.

"May I ask what this is all about?" Amanda's grandmother asked as the second soldier grabbed her.

"How old are you?" he asked Amanda's grandma as he looked over her.

"I'm seventy-nine," she answered through clenched teeth. Her legs shook, and her heart pounded. The soldier could see the fear in her eyes, but his heart was numb to her feelings. He had psyched himself up for this mission and he was going to do his job.

"Come with me," Sgt. Lewis said to Amanda as he pushed her to the door. Amanda's grandmother tried to go too.

"You stay here!" shouted the other soldier and pushed her to the floor.

"Granny!"

Amanda cried as Sgt. Lewis pushed her outside the door. Amanda cried as her legs gave way and she went lame to the ground. The two soldiers dragged her to one of the trucks and threw her in. Her grandmother struggled to get up on her feet.

Steve ran downstairs and fell on his knees beside his grandmother. She grabbed her chest.

"Call the paramedics son," she said through clenched teeth. Steve jumped up and ran to the phone and dialed 911, but only a recording replied.

"All circuits are busy now. Please try to call again later." Steve ran outside and shouted for help.

"Help! Help my grandmother!" he screamed. One of the soldiers hit him in the face with the butt of his gun. Steve fell to the ground and slightly lost consciousness as the commotion went on around him.

Amanda screamed as she tried to get out of the truck.

"Sit down lady! If you know what's good for you," a soldier said.

"My brother is hurt! Please let me see him!" Amanda cried. An older woman from the back of the truck got up and grabbed Amanda by the arm and pulled her to the back of the truck.

"Why are they doing this? What did we do?" Amanda cried.

"Lady if I have to come back there!" the soldier raised his voice.

"Keep quiet now. Everything is going to be all right," the lady said. Amanda could no longer see outside from the back of the truck. She just sat there with her hand over her mouth sobbing. The soldiers threw a few more women in the truck. Amanda thought she recognized one of the girls from school. She looked again and it was Felicia.

Everything was spinning when Steve got up. He looked down the street as the trucks drove away.

"Are you all right son?" a man asked as he helped Steve get on his feet. "It's my grandmother. I think she's having a heart attack."

"Where is she?" the man asked.

"Over there," Steve said as he pointed to the house. The man ran inside the house and Steve followed. His grandmother was lying on the floor.

"Ma'am," the man called as he kneeled down beside her.

"What hurts, ma'am?" he asked.

"It's my back. I can't move."

Steve and the man helped her up and laid her on the couch. Steve began to cry.

"It's okay Steve. It will take a lot to get rid of me," his grandmother said, forcing a smile.

"They took Amanda, grandma," Steve said as he cried. "They put her in a truck and drove away."

"I know son," his granny said as she raised her hand and put it on his cheek.

"Do you know what's going on?" she asked the man.

"I don't know. They took my wife and daughter. Something about a government experiment, but we are going downtown to demand some answers," he said, pulse boiling.

"I want answers too. They took my Amanda. They just walked in and took her," granny said.

"I heard everything from upstairs," Steve told the man.

"My daughter was only six," the man said through clenched teeth.

Steve's eyes widened. "I want answers too. We have to get them back," he said.

"We will, son," his grandmother said as she groaned and turned over on her back.

"Granny, are you okay?"

"I'll be fine. I just have to rest," she said as she closed her eyes.

"Granny! Granny!" Steve cried as he shook his grandmother. The man checked her pulse and shook his head.

"She's gone," he said.

"No," Steve cried as he fell across his grandmother.

"I'm sorry, son," the man said.

"She was old. It was too much excitement for her. Do you have anyone else you could contact?"

"No. Just my sister and they took her," Steve sobbed.

"Do you have a sheet or blanket?"

"I can get you a sheet." Steve ran upstairs and got a sheet. He came back downstairs and handed it to the man.

"I'm John by the way," the man said. "You are welcome to come with me."

He placed the sheet over Steve's grandmother's body.

"There is nothing more we could do for her now," he said.

Steve looked at the TV and there was an emergency broadcast on. It declared martial law. People rioted on the streets, broken in stores and businesses. Helicopters flew overhead and policemen with riot gear and dogs tried to control the situation.

Steve got his baseball bat, ran out into the crowd and began to shout at the police. The police shot teargas into the crowd and released their dogs. Young boys threw rocks and bottles at the police. The rioting lasted way over into the morning. Buildings and businesses had burned. The National Guard came and began shooting in the crowd. People ran in all directions. Steve went back to his house where his grandma's lifeless body lay on the couch. He kneeled down beside her and began to cry. John came back. "Come with me son," he said.

Amanda sat in the back of the truck with her hand over her mouth sobbing, when Felicia saw her. She made her way to the back and sat down.

"Amanda Richardson? Is that you?" Amanda looked up and nodded her head yes.

"Are you okay? Are you hurt?" Felicia asked.

"No, it's my grandmother. I think she's hurt and my brother was just lying there on the street," Amanda said.

"They just stormed in my house and shot my father and took me and my sister. They took my mother too," said Felicia.

"What's going on?" Amanda asked.

"I don't know, but for some time now there have been some rumors about a government experiment," Felicia said.

"An experiment?"

"Yes, and they want to experiment on black women."

Amanda thought about what Felicia had said. "An experiment? What experiment? These experiments could kill me. I'll never be able to go to Harvard or any other college. I worked hard all my life to go to Harvard and now I won't be able to. My grandmother, she needs me and she might be hurt. Steve was hurt and he was left lying there on the street. I got to get off this truck," she thought to herself.

She looked at Felicia who was also deep in her thoughts.

"We have to get off this truck," Amanda said.

"But how, Amanda? There are three soldiers up there with guns. They will shoot us," Felicia said.

Amanda began to cry.

"Hey, lady," an older woman sitting next to Felicia whispered.

"We can get off this truck if we all work together. We could overpower the soldiers. We might have a chance," the lady said.

"I'll act like I'm hurt and when the guard comes back, we all jump on him and take his gun," the lady said. Amanda's eyes widened. She wanted to get off the truck, but she didn't want to get hurt. She wanted to go back to her granny in one piece.

Amanda's heart started racing as she listened to the women talk. She looked to the front of the truck and saw that the soldiers were talking. It looked as though they weren't paying attention. Amanda began to think that they might have a chance. She closed her eyes, said a little prayer, and crossed her fingers. The woman looked at Amanda.

"Are you ready?" she asked.

"We all have to be ready. We have to move fast," the lady said.

"We are ready," Felicia said.

Amanda nodded her head yes. The lady stood up and collapsed on the floor of the truck. Sgt. Lewis looked back and grabbed his gun.

"All right, what's going on here?" he asked.

"She collapsed!" the women screamed.

Sgt. Lewis got up and walked to the back of the truck. The women jumped on him. The other two soldiers pulled out their tasers and began tasing the women. They all fell numb on the floor of the truck. Amanda didn't move. She just sat there eyes wide, her heart beating fast. She watched Felicia get stunned. She lay there, slobbering.

"You women want to play games?" Sgt. Lewis asked.

"We are not here to play games with you. We are here to take you to your destination and that's what we are going to do. Now you could go there the easy way and all you have to do is cooperate, sit and remain quiet, or you could go the hard way. That's in a body bag. One way or another, you will get there."

The lady came to her senses and sat up.

"You. Come with me," Sgt. Lewis said as he grabbed her by the arm and walked her to the front of the truck. Amanda shook Felicia who was still dazed from the taser.

"Felicia are you okay?" Amanda asked.

Felicia just lay there, numb.

"We are never going to get away," Amanda whispered. "They would never let us go. What do they want from us? It seems like an eternity since we've been on this truck."

Amanda lost track of time. She didn't know where they were or how to get back to Chicago. She had never been out of Chicago before. She had never even been to the suburbs, but she knew she wasn't in Chicago anymore.

Where was she? She didn't know.

"Where are they taking us? To a hospital or clinic? What kind of treatment are we going to receive?" she thought. She sat back, closed her eyes and tried to relax, but her grandmother came in her thoughts and the image of Steve just lying there on the ground. She began to sob.

"My grandmother," she cried. She wasn't worried about herself; she worried about her grandmother and Steve. Who was going to take care of them?

The truck made a turn and changed terrain like it was driving on a gravel road. The light in front of the truck got dark. Amanda's heart began to beat faster. Felicia sat up.

"What happened?" Felicia asked, her speech slurred.

"They stunned you with a taser," Amanda said. Felicia's head was spinning. It felt like she wanted to throw up. She felt between her legs and she felt wet. She had relieved herself.

"I think we are almost there. The truck changed direction," Amanda said.

It hit a couple of bumps and Amanda knew that they weren't on pavement anymore. Thoughts raced through her head and her mouth became dry. She bit her lip. Sgt. Lewis stood up.

"We are almost there," he said smiling. He walked to the back of the truck and looked at Felicia who seemed dazed and confused. He snapped his finger in her face.

"Wake up. You're almost there," he said.

Amanda's heart raced and tears rolled down her face. The truck slowed down and Amanda could hear other men directing the truck. Amanda tightened her fist and held her breath. The truck stopped and Sgt. Lewis jumped out. They opened the door and began pulling the women out.

CHAPTER

They pulled Amanda out of the truck and made her stand in a long line. She looked ahead of her and saw four large tents and people in biohazard suits like on TV. They were examining the black women, laying them on gurneys, and waving a strange instrument over their bodies. They then took them to the next tent and gave them some kind of shot. The line was moving fast.

It was almost Amanda's turn. Her heart started pounding as if it was going to jump out of her chest. Her legs felt weak. She turned around to get out of line, but a soldier shoved her back.

"Keep the line moving!" he said.

Amanda looked at Felicia who tried to fight back. They forced her on to the gurney, gave her some kind of shot in her neck, and she was out. The other women gasped when they saw what happened to Felicia and so they began to cooperate. They went willingly to the exam.

A man in one of the suits came and grabbed Amanda by the arm. Amanda's eyes widened as she walked slowly with the man. He lay her on the gurney and waved the instrument over her body, from her head to her toe. The instrument read: Temperature 97, Blood pressure 120/70, Pulse 102.

Her vitals were normal and there were no signs of disease.

"This is a healthy one. Take her to the next tent," the man said.

They took her off the stretcher and brought her to the next tent. Amanda's heart was racing and her knees became weaker. She could hardly walk to the other tent, but the soldiers snatched her by the arm.

"Come on, get moving," one of them said.

In the other tent, they gave her six shots using some kind of gun needle. Amanda felt the medicine go through her. It was a warm sensation. They took her to another tent and told her to take off her clothes.

Amanda hesitated because they were all men. But she took them off, and they gave her some clean underwear, a gray jumpsuit, some socks and a pair of tennis shoes. They told her to put them on.

Afterwards, they took her to another tent where they gave her a tray of food and a glass of Kool-Aid and directed her to sit down. She sat down and looked at the food. Whatever was in that shot made her hungry. Another girl sat down beside her. Amanda looked up. It was Hope, a girl from her homeroom class at school.

Hope's hands were trembling and it looked as though she had been crying.

"Were you in the truck with me?" Amanda asked.

"I don't know. A soldier hit me with the butt of his gun and put me in the truck. When I woke up, I was here. My head did hurt, but it's fine now. But, I am hungry," Hope said.

Amanda looked down at her tray. It looked like some kind of meat, potatoes, coleslaw, and a roll. She tasted the meat; it was like meatloaf. The gravy, like beef gravy. She ate it in three bites. She then drank the Kool-Aid.

Amanda sat there and watched the other women and saw how they began to cooperate. She looked around to see if there was some way to escape, but behind the tents was a cluster of trees, and soldiers were watching the women while they ate.

The women finished their food. But suddenly, a soldier in a strange blue uniform that Amanda didn't recognize walked up to her and grabbed her by the arm. He blindfolded her and tied her hands together in front of her. Amanda's heart began to pound. When they blindfolded all the women, they led them into the woods through a cluster of trees and into a large room.

They told them to sit on the floor. When all the women got into the room, they told them to take off their blindfold. Amanda took off her blindfold and looked around the room. It was enormous even though it had almost ten million women in it. It was not crowded or cramped. The room was white and very bright. There were no windows or doors.

The women began to talk and it sounded like a crowd in a football stadium, but in a hollow tunnel. Amanda looked in a row in front of her and saw Hope sitting there. Hope looked back at Amanda. When Amanda was about to say something, a man in a strange uniform came into the room. He walked up to a podium in front of them.

The women stopped talking when they saw him. The room was so quiet one could hear a pin drop. Amanda's heart pounded as she looked at the tall lean man at the podium. He was an olive-skinned man. Amanda thought that he was probably Hispanic, but his clothes looked funny. The women were quiet as he looked at them. He smiled and raised his hand.

"Welcome," he said in a strange accent. "I am Colonel Bardolph Galveston and I want to welcome you aboard my ship." The women gasped and looked around.

"We are going on a journey to what I hope will be your new home, for those who cooperate. You will become part of our society where you will be able to have a family, a job, and an education. Most of you will live much like how you lived on Earth, but you will be crossbred with our men and make a new and stronger hybrid race."

"Are you going to enslave us?" one of the women asked.

"Heavens no, you will have rights and privileges just like any other Malatha citizen. If you simply cooperate and not try to escape or break any laws."

"But, I already have a husband," a lady from the back said.

"You will have a new husband," Galveston replied, laughing. "Remember your only purpose is to crossbreed and make a new race of Malatha children. Now we are going to divide you up in groups and take you to your sections. We should arrive in Malatha in a week, Earth time."

When he stepped down, they began putting the women into groups. They took them to their sleeping quarters. Amanda and Hope shared a room since two persons can occupy one room. The room had a bathroom, two beds, a chest of drawers, a nightstand, and a mirror.

The soldier in charge of the section gave them a plastic bag with toiletries. It had a toothbrush, toothpaste, soap, and a comb. Amanda took her shower first then she went to bed. She tried to sleep, but images of her grandmother went through her mind. She wondered what was going to happen to them. She couldn't believe that this was happening. Was this a dream? She closed her eyes and a calm came over her.

Lieutenant Aiden Baxter was writing his report and typing the list of names of the women who belonged to his section on his computer. He was the officer in charge of Section C775. He was pleased that everything went according to plan today. He was impressed with the US Military. He didn't expect that such a primitive race could be so efficient. He wrote about Col. Jackson and how he accommodated the needs of his colonel well. The US Military met their demands without incident.

"It's not like they weren't going to get anything out of it. We paid them well. Who wouldn't want a cure for cancer and HIV? And technology for a new fighter plane? Even though the technology is primitive by our standards," he thought to himself.

Once the women got over their fear, things began to go smoothly.

"I think the women will make an excellent addition to the Malatha way of life," Aiden thought. He thought about a book he had read about the African-American women in his anthropology class. They are very religious, musically-inclined, and athletic. But they could be very superstitious. They had been through a lot throughout history and because of that they are strong and could bounce back from anything. That's what he wanted in a wife, a strong, well-rounded, and talented woman who could live up to the challenge.

Ever since Aiden was a boy, the Malatha government had been talking about taking the African-American women and bringing them to Malatha where they could be brides for the Malatha males. They had been planning this for many years. Aiden thought that that was a good idea. He wanted a female companion, someone he could love and trust and share his life with. That's one of the reasons he joined the military, so he could be part of the mission to retrieve the women. He was excited when he was chosen out of a hundred candidates to be Col. Galveston's assistant.

He had worked hard to be the best pilot and combat commander in his class. He had studied all he could about Earth, the United States, and the African-American women, and became an expert. He finished typing and he looked over his work. He was pleased with what he wrote and leaned back in his chair to stretch. He closed his eyes and began to relax. Sgt. Piers Durandel rang his bell. Aiden opened his eyes and sat up.

"Come in," he said. The door slid back and Sgt. Durandel came in and saluted. Aiden saluted back.

"At ease, sergeant," he said.

"Thank you, sir. The women are all in their quarters. Everything went according to plan. There wasn't any incident. The monitor shows that they are all asleep. I have a good feeling about this sir," Durandel said.

"Oh, how so?" Aiden asked.

"Well at first the women were afraid, but after Col. Galveston talked to them, they calmed down and even began to laugh and talk. I know some of the women are a little apprehensive but give them a little time. They will come around." "You think so?" Aiden asked.

"Yes, sir. It's just one person I'm a little worried about. It might be nothing. I mean it's nothing I can't handle." "What is it, sergeant? " Aiden asked.

"It's this girl. She's no more than 18 years old. C7752. Her name is Felicia. She tried to fight back when we examined her. She fought back again when we took her to her quarters. She won't cooperate. All of the other women are fine. When it was time for lights out, she kept talking to her roommate and it seems to me her roommate wants to cooperate. I want permission to put her in one of the cells until we reach Malatha if she doesn't shape up tomorrow. You know, one bad apple. "I know sergeant. You do what you think is best."

"Thank you, sir," Sgt. Durandel said as he saluted Aiden.

"Good night, sir," he said as he turned and walked out of the door.

Aiden looked up C7752 on his computer and made a note by her name, a good candidate for Infusement Treatment. He looked at her picture but felt no connection with her. So, he scanned down the list. He turned off his computer and looked at the time. It was nine in the morning on Malatha. So, he called his mother. Abigail Baxter came on the screen.

"How did everything go Aiden?" she asked smiling, excited to hear from him.

"Everything went well. We have all the women. There weren't any casualties and we didn't have to fight. We just exchanged some information for the women and we were off." "I'm glad," Abigail said.

"Where is dad?"

"Oh, he went into the office early today, but I'll tell him you called. I can't wait until the women get here. It'll make things so much interesting around here. I'm glad you are well, son."

"I'm glad you are too, mom," Aiden said smiling.

"I'll see you Friday."

"Okay, son. Goodbye," Abigail said.

"Goodbye," Aiden pressed End Call and got up from his desk. He touched a button on a panel on the wall and turned on some light music. It was like a soft symphony of string instruments. He began to lose himself in the music when an alarm went off.

"An intruder!" The computer said.

"An intruder?" Aiden's heart began to race and his eyes widened. He grabbed his phaser and ran out of the door. Sgt. Durandel and two other soldiers with phasers ready met him in the hall. They looked on a panel on the wall and saw that the intruder was in the observation lounge. Aiden pressed a button locking down the door to the lounge. They went down to the lounge and Sgt. Durandel and the other two soldiers went in. It was Felicia. She had gone out of her room and was wandering in the halls. Sgt. Durandel grabbed her by the arm and walked out of the lounge. He walked up to Aiden.

"This is the one I told you about."

Aiden looked down at her. She was a short stout dark-skinned girl with braids.

"Who was supposed to guard the security monitors?" Aiden asked.

"Jacks," Durandel said.

"Where is he? Why didn't he see C7752?"

"I don't know."

"Put her in a cell for the remainder of the trip. She has to see Chancellor De Ivory. Where is Jacks?"

Aiden walked over to the security monitors and Jacks was there, nodding off.

"Jacks, are you supposed to be on duty?"

Jacks jumped up and saluted.

"Yes, sir."

"Why are you nodding?"

"I'm sorry, sir but I didn't get much sleep today. I worked a double for Elliott, and he was supposed to work for me today, but he didn't show up, sir."

"Computer, where is Elliott?" Aiden asked.

"Elliott is in the viewing lounge," the computer said.

"Elliott, get to security monitors section C775, now! Aiden called.

CHAPTER

Amanda woke up before Hope. She jumped out of bed and grabbed her plastic bag of toiletries. She walked over to the chest of drawers, grabbed a set of towels, and went into the bathroom. She turned on the water to the shower. She turned it on hot and let it run. She looked into the mirror and pulled her hair back off her shoulders.

She pinned it up and took off her clothes. She checked the water and it was just right. She stepped into the shower, washed all over, thinking of her grandmother. She would never see them again, she thought as a numb feeling hit her chest. What is going to happen to them? Are they safe back there on Earth?

She thought about Steve. He is just a boy. Tears rolled down her cheeks as she wiped them away with her towel. She stepped out of the shower, wrapped the towel around her, and walked into the room. Hope woke up and sat up in bed.

"Is it time to get up?" she asked.

"I'm not sure. I couldn't sleep anymore. So, I took a shower," Amanda said.

"How is the water?" Hope asked.

"It's warm," Amanda said as she put on her jumpsuit.

Hope got up and went into the bathroom. Amanda let down her hair and combed it in the mirror. Her hair was shoulder length and she wore bangs. She put on her shoes and began making her bed when the lights came on. Soft music began to play in the intercom.

"Good morning, ladies," a voice over the intercom said.

"I'm Chancellor De Ivory. I would be your Minister of Adjustment throughout your stay with us on Malatha. We understand that you have a lot to learn about our way of life and we know that moving to a new place could be intimidating and challenging. So, we are going to try to make your stay on my Malatha as pleasant as possible. Each section will have adjustment training where you will learn about the Malatha way of life. After breakfast you will be instructed what to do. Again, good morning and welcome."

Amanda listened as she made her bed.

"Minister of Adjustment," she said.

Hope came out of the bathroom fully dressed.

"Are they going to train us how to live on Malatha?" she asked.

"That's what he said."

"This is getting stranger and stranger," Amanda said as she threw her arms up.

"I know. I was lying in bed hoping that this was a bad dream," Hope said.

"I was too. Until I opened my eyes and looked around," Amanda said.

The door slid open and Sgt. Durandel came in.

"Good morning ladies. Are you ready to have breakfast? Our section will meet with Chancellor De Ivory after breakfast. Here is everything you need," he continued as he handed them two touchscreen tablets.

"Come with me," he said.

The two women walked out of their quarters and out into the hall. The hall was bright with silver metallic walls and a maroon carpet. There was a panel of buttons and a viewing screen on the wall. The ship was warm about seventy degrees Fahrenheit and the other women in their section were in the hall waiting.

The women walked down the long hall and into the dining lounge. The dining lounge was large with round tables and it had large windows revealing what was outside the ship.

Amanda was amazed to see the darkness of space and the cluster of stars. It was just like TV. There was a long counter in front of the lounge with a long buffet of food. The aroma of the food marched up Amanda's nose and her stomach rumbled with hunger. She immediately went over and picked up a tray and began placing food on it.

It was so much food to choose from Amanda couldn't decide; it was a feast fit for a queen. Aiden was sitting at the table across from the buffet. He looked up and saw Amanda. She was tall and graceful, her body was slender, her hips slim, her skin was like milk chocolate smooth as silk. She glided across the dining lounge floor as if she was floating on air.

Aiden watched her as she sat down, crossed her legs, and tasted her food. Her face was a perfect oval, and her lips were rounded over even teeth. Aiden's heart jolted as he gave her body a reckoning gaze. He knew at that moment he had to have her.

Amanda liked the food she was eating. It was some kind of eggs and sausages, but it didn't taste like chicken eggs or pork sausage, but it tasted good to Amanda. The coffee was still coffee and she drowned it with cream and sugar.

Aiden watched her slender fingers stir her coffee slowly. She stirred the coffee with a spoon and slowly raised it to her mouth, tasting it. What care she gave to the task of stirring, Aiden thought. She tantalized his senses and an arousing sensation went through Aiden's manhood. He started panting and he had to exhale for air.

Aiden made a mental note of her identification number: C77554. He had to hurry up and claim her in the match office before someone else did. He knew she was the one he dreamed about at night. He was ready to spend the rest of his life with her. He got up and slowly walked over to Amanda as she drank her coffee.

He stopped in front of her and Amanda looked up at Aiden. He stood tall and straight like a towering gladiator. His muscles were rippling under his blue uniform, it quickened her pulse. She looked up at his powerful set of shoulders and her heart melted. He stood there devilishly handsome. Amanda's eyes froze on his light olive complexion and his black hair gleamed in the light.

"Hi, my name is Lieutenant Aiden Baxter," his accent was odd but gentle.

He reached for her hand to shake it.

"What is your name?" he asked.

"I'm Amanda," she answered over her beating heart.

She placed her hand in his hand and he trembled with eagerness. Her hand was soft like a rose petal.

"I'm the commanding officer in this section. Did you have enough to eat?" Aiden asked smiling, his teeth were straight and white.

"Yes," Amanda answered eagerly.

"Do you have any questions?" he asked. He wanted to know what she was thinking.

"What part of Malatha are you taking us?" Amanda asked smiling.

Aiden was surprised that she thought about such things.

"That's a good question," he said smiling. "Malatha is divided into seven continents, that's why we divided you up into seven groups. You are going to Gual. It's a tropical continent. Its climate is different from Chicago. It has a lot of sandy beaches and coconuts." "I see, like Hawaii?" Amanda asked.

Aiden thought for a moment. "Yes, much like Hawaii."

Amanda smiled. For a moment, Aiden took her mind off her grandmother.

For two days Aiden had been thinking about Amanda. He could see her innocent eyes looking at him. They pierced his soul like summer lightning. He tried to focus on his work, but something kept nudging him to meet with Chancellor De Ivory. He typed the last of his report on his computer and turned it off. He stepped over to the window and looked out into space.

"Are you sure Aiden? You know if you choose now you can't change your mind later," he thought.

"I have to be absolutely sure."

He thought about Amanda's shapely lips and full figure, and his heart melted.

"I'm sure," he said. Now all he has to do is to petition for her in Chancellor De Ivory's office.

He went to his computer and brought up the law that was pertaining to women. In Article One, Section Two, it stated that all military personnel who were involved in the mission of obtaining the women had the right to choose first. Commissioned officers first, then enlisted personnel.

Aiden wanted to look over the laws once more to confirm that he had the right to make his decision now and he did. A funny feeling came over him.

"After today, I won't be single anymore. I can't believe I actually want to do this," he thought.

He turned off his computer and stood up. He grabbed his utility belt and put it on. He walked out the door and down the hall. He stopped at the security desk where Sgt. Durandel was stationed.

"I'm going down to Chancellor De Ivory's office. I should be back in an hour," Aiden said.

"Yes sir," Sgt. Durandel said as he saluted him.

Aiden walked to the elevator and pressed deck two. The elevator went down to deck two. Chancellor De Ivory had just completed his last meeting with the women today. He was pleased that everything went well. He had a good feeling about his new citizens. They were fast and eager learners. He walked around his desk and turned on his computer. He had a long report to write and he wanted to be as accurate and thorough as possible.

The majority of the women were enthusiastic, and they were willing to learn. They asked the right questions and were obedient in doing what he asked them to do. They were eager to please. He noticed a little apprehension in some of the women, but they tried to participate. Just give them a little time, and they will come around, he thought.

He looked up C77552, Felicia, and read the report that Aiden had written about her. He had planned to meet with her after dinner. Aiden said she was uncontrollable and refused to cooperate. He recommended that she would be a good candidate for infusement treatment.

Chancellor De Ivory didn't want to result to that. He wanted to try to get through to her by talking to her. He found that women were much more enjoyable using their own thoughts and personality. Infusement treatment was for hardened prisoners who had a hard time fitting into society. It was only used as a last resort.

It was harsh and painful. If Felicia lived through it, she would be like a robot with no feelings or personality of her own. Chancellor De Ivory's bell rang and he looked up at the door.

"Come in," he said.

Aiden stepped in and walked up to his desk.

"Yes, may I help you?" De Ivory asked.

Aiden hesitated then he spoke up.

"Sir, I want to put in a petition for my pick right now."

De Ivory looked wide-eyed at Aiden.

"So soon, son. Are you sure?"

"Yes, sir," Aiden said, thinking of Amanda.

"So, you know that the law states that if you choose now you can't change your mind later? So that means you are stuck with your decision unless she held a severe illness or death."

"I'm well aware of that sir," Aiden said. "I'm sure."

"Are you? How long have you been thinking about this, son?"

"For quite some time now, sir. I thought long and hard about it and I am a hundred percent sure."

De Ivory looked at Aiden for a long while.

"Who is this lucky lady?" he finally asked.

"It's C77554," Aiden said smiling.

De Ivory brought her file up on the screen. He looked at her picture and then he looked at Aiden.

"She is a beauty," he said.

"Have you spoken to her?" he asked. "I spoke to her today," Aiden said. "I want you to be absolutely sure."

"I'm sure, sir, and I know it is my right. I can choose right now if I want."

De Ivory looked wide-eyed at Aiden. He was surprised at his frankness.

He smiled.

"All right son, sit down."

Aiden sat down and de Ivory brought the contract up on the computer screen.

"You know son," he said eyebrows raised. "You are the first to come down."

Aiden smiled.

"I wanted to beat the crowd."

De Ivory laughed and read him the contract.

Aiden listened carefully but he knew what was on the contract because he had read it himself in his quarters. De Ivory emphasized the part about not being able to change his mind, but Aiden didn't bulge. He was ready. "All right son, sign here."

Aiden signed the computer pad.

"You are all set. We will have Amanda ready for you to take home on Friday. Go to the meeting hall at the capital pavilion and she would be waiting."

"Thank you, sir," Aiden replied, feeling good about his decision.

He had decided not to see her anymore until Friday to make that day much more special. He walked out of De Ivory's office and down the hall to the elevator. He was no longer single. He was spoken for. Now he could have the son he always wanted.

He could teach him things like, how to swim, and drive. He could talk to him about life. Like his father did to him. His dreams were coming true. He didn't know what he would do when that day came. Now it was here and he was amazed that he was taking it so well. He looked at the time. He had to call his father. His father would be proud. He always supported him in his decisions.

CHAPTER

The Malatha vessel had orbited the planet. Aiden's father was waiting at the ship port for him. Aiden came down on a space shuttle and met his father at the port. His father was a tall slender man with salt and pepper hair, and a little gray in his beard. He looked like an older Aiden.

"Dad, did you get my message?" Aiden asked as he hugged his father.

"Yes, son."

"I'm sorry I kept missing you, but I got tied up at the office. But I'm happy for you," Aaron said as he patted Aiden on the back.

"She is really pretty, dad. She's nice too. You'll like her. She's intelligent. We talked a couple of times before I made up my mind. She stole my heart, dad," Aiden said.

Aaron looked at his son. He saw how happy he was. He knew he wanted a relationship for a long time and when he found out he was assigned to the mission to go to Earth, he was happy. Aaron and his mother were concerned about the mission. They didn't want Aiden to be deployed so far away, but Aiden wanted to go. So against their better judgment, they let him go.

"I'm so happy for you, son," Aaron said. "Where is she?"

"They are taking her to the meeting hall in the capital pavilion. I have to go and pick her up at four o'clock."

Aiden and his father went to a bar near the capital pavilion. They sat down at the bar and ordered some beers.

"So, tell me everything, son. How did you meet? Where was she when you first saw her? What is she like?"

Aiden looked at his father and laughed.

"Slow down."

"I'm sorry. I'm just so happy for you. I have a million questions," Aaron said laughing.

"She was in the dining lounge when I first saw her. She walked in and went up to the counter and got her breakfast. And then she glided across the floor to her seat and sat down so gracefully. She is tall and slender with milk chocolate complexion. She has long black hair and big brown eyes. She's smart too. We had a very meaningful conversation the other day. I feel like I can confide in her," Aiden paused.

"It's just I sense a bit of sadness in her. I don't know what it is. It may be the way she was taken and made to come here. She lost her family, her home, and her planet. I want to comfort her and show her that everything is going to be all right."

"You have to let her know that we are her family now. From what I read about those people, they are very resilient. Give her a little time."

"Does she like you?" Aaron added.

Aiden looked at his father.

"Yes, I can sense it. She always greeted me with a smile."

The bartender brought them another beer.

"Were you with that away team who brought back all of those women?" he asked Aiden looking at his uniform.

"Yes," Aiden said.

"Are they here? I want to petition for a wife when they passed the ordinance. I thought that it was a good idea. Prime Minister Castor Raincourt should be rewarded because things were getting desperate around here. When can I put in my petition?" the bartender asked.

"As soon as possible," Aiden answered.

"Well, I better do it soon before all the good ones are gone!"

Aiden laughed.

"There are plenty to go around. We have over twenty million women and girls."

"How young do they range from?" the bartender asked.

"Infant to sixty, but the young ones are going to stay with their mothers until they are old enough to marry."

"That's good. We wouldn't want to separate the women from their children," the bartender said. Aiden drank his beer.

"No, we tried not to."

"It would be nice to have a woman's touch around here. We have to open up shops, beauty shops, schools for the kids, and clinics just to name a few. That means more jobs. It's a win-win situation," the bartender said.

"Yes, will have a full functioning society," Aaron said.

Aiden looked at his watch and his heart jolted. He looked at his father.

"It's time," he said.

His father's eyes widened and he smiled.

"Time? Time for what?" the bartender asked.

"I'm going to pick up my wife," Aiden said smiling. The bartender smiled too.

"You lucky devil, congrats. Where is she?"

"She's at the pavilion."

"I have to go pick her up at four o'clock."

"Well, you better get a move on! It's only a quarter 'til four. You don't want to keep her waiting."

"Oh, I won't."

Aiden drank the last of his beer. His father placed his hands on his chest and exhaled.

"Well, this is it," he said.

"Let's go."

They stood up and walked out of the bar. They walked across the street to the pavilion and walked inside. It was a large white marble building with large white columns and marble floors. It had stone statues of their past prime ministers and pictures of their founding fathers on the wall. The meeting hall was on the first floor and Aiden and his father opened up the door and walked in.

It was a large arena with rows of seats going down to the bottom and a platform. Aiden walked down to the platform and Mrs. De Balon, an old Malatha woman, was seated in one of the chairs near the platform.

"May I help you?" she asked.

"I'm Lieutenant Aiden Baxter. I'm here to see Chancellor De Ivory.

She looked on her tablet for his name.

"Baxter, oh, here you are. You are his four o'clock. He's not quite ready yet. Please have a seat."

Amanda's heart raced when Chancellor De Ivory told her that she was chosen. She put her hand over her mouth in disbelief. Who could this be? She thought. For the past week when she was on the ship, she didn't notice any men, only a few soldiers here and there. Who could have noticed her? She bit her lip.

"I can't get married. I'm too young, and most of all, I'm not in love!" she said angrily.

When the ship reached Malatha, Durandel and a group of other soldiers gathered the women and took them to the shuttle bay. They put them on a large space shuttle and flew them to the surface of Malatha. The shuttle landed in a large grassy field with bright yellow flowers.

The soldiers transferred the women to several large vehicles. They took them to a compound in the hills of Gaul. The windows were tinted, but Amanda could see a very beautiful countryside filled with large fields with hills, grass, and trees.

There was an occasional house here and there, and to Amanda's surprise, the houses were made of glass and steel and looked very futuristic like the houses in a science fiction magazine, unlike the houses on Earth. When they got to the compound, the soldiers divided the women into groups of twos and took them to a three-story building where they stayed until they were called for.

The women lived two to a room much like they were on the ship. The compound was surrounded by a large electric force field which kept the women from wandering off the grounds of the compound. Chancellor De Ivory got Amanda and put her in a hovercar. Amanda was amazed that they had that technology. He took her to the city of Surrok. The city downtown area was big with towering skyscrapers, businesses, and shops. The streets were filled with men walking in and out of the businesses.

There was multi-lane traffic filled with hovercars, and the traffic was bumper-to-bumper. The streets were paved with concrete much like on Earth. There were light posts, trash cans, and neon signs on buildings just like those in New York.

The car passed a side street and Amanda looked down from it and saw the ocean. It was big and blue just like the Pacific Ocean. So, their city was near the ocean, Amanda thought. The sky was clear, and the sun shined brightly down on the car.

There wasn't any shade. It was incredibly warm and humid it felt like it was a hundred degrees. There was a little park and men were sitting on the ground talking under the sun. Some men were jogging and riding bikes.

Amanda was amazed at the similarities to Earth. But there were no women, she thought. She saw restaurants with tables and umbrellas along the sidewalks. There was a large water fountain with a statue of two Malatha animals embraced in a kiss. Amanda thought of the Buckingham Fountain in Chicago. Amanda could hear the crowd of men talking, footsteps walking, and the motor of the hovercars. The car stopped in front of the capital pavilion and Chancellor De Ivory and Amanda got out.

They walked into the building and down a long corridor to the meeting hall. Chancellor De Ivory took Amanda to a dressing room at the back of the hall. Two older Malatha women were waiting for them. They were dressed in long silk gowns with embroidery on them.

"This is Acelina and Thora. They are going to get you ready for your mate," De Ivory said smiling.

"Now I'm going to the other room, so you can get ready."

Amanda grabbed him by the arm and began to cry.

"No, don't leave me," she said.

De Ivory's eyes widened as he tried to wiggle free.

"I have to go, Amanda. You have to get ready," he said.

"No, I don't want to get married," Amanda cried. "Why me?"

"You were chosen. Consider yourself lucky. Remember what we told you. Your only purpose here is to be a bride, and a beautiful bride you will be."

"No, I won't!" Amanda cried as she held on tighter to De Ivory.

"Give me a little more time," she sobbed.

"I'm sorry Amanda, but you are a big girl now. Today is your day. You will make a good wife. Your mate is a good man. He has a lot to offer you. You will be well taken care of. So, stop this!" De Ivory shouted firmly. "Stop this now and let those women get you ready!"

Amanda let go of him and wiped her tears. She looked wide-eyed at De Ivory.

"Now you get ready and I'll be back in half an hour to get you."

Acelina grabbed her by the arm and led her to the mirror. They pulled out a long maroon gown from a box and Amanda began taking off her clothes. Amanda exhaled and put on the embroidered gown that was prepared for her. They let down her hair and let it flow down her shoulders. Amanda looked at herself in the mirror and she thought she looked like a girl from India.

Aiden and his father had been waiting for over an hour.

"Could you tell me what the problem is?" he asked De Balon.

"There was a slight complication, but we got it resolved. She will be out shortly."

Aiden exhaled and looked at his watch. He patted his foot on the floor. Chancellor De Ivory finally came out.

"Aiden, sorry to keep you waiting but we ran into a slight problem, but she will be out shortly," De Ivory said. Aiden stood up and straightened his uniform.

"I'm sorry, dad," he said.

"No problem," his father said as he watched Aiden pace.

"Don't worry son. She will be out in a few moments," Aaron said.

The door to the back opened and Chancellor De Ivory stood on the platform.

"Here she is," he said smiling.

Aiden looked up as she approached him. He became quiet as he studied her. The long silk dress hugged her body, revealing her slim hips. Aiden smiled with his eyes. Amanda looked up and saw Aiden. She rejoiced in her heart. Her smile broadened with approval.

Aiden picked her up and swung her around excitedly. Aaron stood up and grinned. Aiden put her down happily.

"Isn't she beautiful, dad?" he asked.

Amanda looked at Aaron with her big brown eyes.

"She's gorgeous. I'm proud of you, son," Aaron said.

Chancellor De Ivory stepped down from the platform and walked up to Aiden.

"You made an excellent choice, son. I wish you the best. I hope you and Amanda have a long prosperous life together. A life filled with adventure and love, and have lots of children."

"We will, sir. Thank you for everything," Aiden said.

"You are welcome, son," De Ivory said. "Well, Amanda this is it. See? I told you that you will be happy." "I am," Amanda said smiling.

De Ivory hugged her. He then shook Aiden and Aaron's hands.

"Aiden, I will see you at work on Monday," De Ivory said.

"I'll see you, Chancellor," Aiden replied.

He took Amanda by the hand and they walked out the exit. Aaron followed them. They walked hand and hand through the pavilion. Other Malatha men who were working inside the pavilion saw them. They all stopped and watched Aiden and Amanda pass by.

Aiden felt proud because Amanda was beautiful, and he had the first choice. Amanda felt a little intimidated because she was in a new place. She had never been away from home before, nor has she ever had a relationship with a man. And Aiden, he wasn't human. He wasn't an Earth human.

How is she going to make this work? What would her grandmother say?

"Am I ever going to see her again?" she thought. And that thought frightened her. She held on to Aiden's hand tight. He looked at her and a warm feeling went over him.

Amanda could feel the affection for her. She could see it in his eyes. She was beginning to have affection for him too, but against her better judgment.

"Don't do this Amanda. Don't fall in love. You can't love him," her mind said.

But when she looked at Aiden, her heart overflowed with joy.

Aaron looked at Amanda. He thinks Amanda will make a good wife. She looked intelligent and it seemed she could handle household chores. They look good together. They make a good couple, he thought.

Aiden noticed the look on his father's face.

"We should hurry up and go home. We have to introduce her to mom," he said.

"I know. She is dying to meet her," Aaron said.

CHAPTER 6

When Aaron pulled into the driveway, Aiden turned to Amanda. "This is your new home," he said.

Amanda's eyes widened and her heart overflowed. It was a beautiful large rectangular glass-steel house that sat on two acres of land. The land was beautiful. It was filled with lots of grass, trees, and flowers. There was a pool in the backyard and a patio with lawn furniture, a gazebo and a wooden swing dangling from a large tree.

Aiden took her inside the glasshouse and the big and spacious living room greeted them. The living room furniture looked expensive. It was in a powder blue shade with lots of pillows. The dining room was like something out of a magazine. It had a large crystal chandelier and a long glass dining table. It can accommodate ten guests.

The kitchen was spacious too, and to Amanda's surprise, the appliances looked similar to Earth. From the kitchen, Aiden took her to another room.

"This is my mother's studio," he said.

Amanda went inside the room and saw oil paintings on the wall. Canvases propped in one corner of the room. Paints and brushes were on the table in the middle of the room. Abigail Baxter was sitting on a stool at an easel, painting a picture of an African-American girl carrying her school books. Amanda had seen that painting before, but she couldn't remember where.

"Mom," Aiden called.

Abigail turned around.

"Oh my god! Aiden, you're home," she said smiling.

"Yes, here she is," Aiden replied, pointing at Amanda.

Abigail smiled and hugged her. Amanda's heart raced and she trembled as she hugged Abigail back.

"Go to the living room while I clean up," Abigail said, waving at them. Aiden took Amanda back to the living room and they sat on the couch.

Aaron went into the kitchen. "Did you cook, honey?" he asked.

"I thought we might go to Sal's Frog Bar tonight. I want to taste some seafood," Abigail said.

She took her smock off and washed her hands. She then stepped into the living room along with Aaron.

"Let me look at you," she said to Amanda. "You are something. How old are you?" "I'm eighteen," Amanda forced out nervously.

"Oh, you are young. When is your birthday?"

"It was in the winter back on Earth. It was in February," Amanda said. "We have to calculate that in Malatha months and years," Abigail said.

"We did that already, mom. Her birthday is on the nineteenth of Luna in the spring. Next Luna, she would be nineteen."

"Well as you know, Aiden is twenty-five. His birthday is in September, in the summer. He's not that much older than you. I think you two would get along fine and make this work. Aaron and I have been married for over thirty years. Right, Aaron?"

Aaron grinned. "Right," he said.

"Well, I got your rooms ready for you. Amanda, you are welcome to whatever it is in the house. The refrigerator is full of food and Aaron has lots of liquor."

Amanda's eyes widened as she looked at Abigail.

"Aiden is a pretty picky eater. So, I will show you how to prepare his favorite dishes. Surrok is a pretty fun city. It has lots of things to do. We have a lot of recreation."

"Yes ma'am," Amanda said.

"Oh, you can call me Abigail."

"Yes, Abigail," Amanda replied, forcing a smile.

"So, tell me about yourself. What did you do on Earth? Where did you live and how did you earn money?"

Amanda's heart pounded as she tried to think of the answers to those questions.

"Well, I lived in Chicago with my grandmother and little brother Steve."

"I was a senior in high school. I was on the honor roll." "Really? You look smart," Abigail said.

"I was chosen to go to the most prestigious university in the country, Harvard."

"Harvard. We've heard of that university. Didn't we dear?" Aaron smiled.

"Yes," he said.

"Well you know Aiden went to the most prestigious military academy in Dacia. Dacia is our mother planet. Did Aiden tell you?" "No," Amanda said.

"Malatha is a colony planet. We all come from Dacia. It's in the same solar system. Well anyway, Aiden went to Dacia Military Academy, where he learned to fly. He's a pilot too. Right, Aiden?" "Yes, mom," Aiden said blushing.

"Well go on, I'm sorry to interrupt."

"I was going to go to Harvard in the fall, but they came and took us. Now I'm here."

Everyone was quiet for a long while.

Aiden looked down. His heart dropped as he felt sorry for Amanda. Abigail's eyes widened as she was at a loss for words. Aaron just stared at her.

"Oh I'm sorry, but if you want you could go to school here. There are a lot of things you could study. Can she, Aiden?"

"Well, she has to go to adjustment training first. They are going to teach her how to read and write. They'll teach her our way of life, but after that, I guess she can go to school. The government is still working on what kind of citizens they are going to be and what kind of rights they will have." "What was going to be your major?" Abigail asked Amanda.

"Medicine," Amanda answered.

"Really?" Abigail said smiling. Well, we could use more doctors around here. Can we Aaron?"

Aaron looked at Abigail.

"Yes, we could. It would take a little longer, but she can do it," he said.

"Well, who's hungry? I thought we might go to Sal's Frog Bar, Aiden. And we can show Amanda downtown," Abigail said smiling.

"That sounds good, mom," Aiden said smiling.

They all stood up. Abigail looked at Amanda and noticed how her hands were trembling. She could sense the fear in her. She smiled and rubbed Amanda on the back in an attempt to make her feel comfortable.

"Sal's Frog Bar is a quaint little place. It's one of my favorites. They serve seafood and steak. You'll love it," Abigail said. "I was thinking maybe you would have the surf and turf. That's one of my favorites." Amanda looked at Abigail.

"Mine too," she said, trying to smile. Her heart was pounding, and waves moved through her stomach. She took a deep breath.

"Get a hold of yourself. Abigail and Aaron seem nice enough. I have to get used to them. I'll be with them for a long time. Well, until I can figure out how to get back home," she thought.

Aiden took her by the hand and a warm feeling went through her. She looked at his ruggedly handsome face. Her heart exploded like bombs and it sang with delight. Aiden thought that everything went well between Amanda and his mother. His mother seems to like her and that was important. Abigail wasn't a hard person to get along with; she just likes to talk. He hoped she didn't make Amanda uncomfortable, he thought as they walked to the door.

"Amanda is a really sweet girl. We have to make her feel at home. I really didn't think about the emotional impact this would have on the women. It's sad," Abigail thought.

They got into the car and Aaron let the top down. The sun was warm on Amanda's face. The countryside was beautiful; it was much prettier than on the west side of Chicago. They drove into town and Amanda looked out at the scenery. She enjoyed her ride. She had never been in a convertible before and the hovercar was smooth it was like floating on air.

They parked their car in the parking lot of the restaurant and went inside. The place was crowded, but Abigail made reservations. The waiter took them to their seats. Everyone stopped and looked when Amanda passed by. The whole place got quiet. Amanda's heart fluttered like running water and she trembled all over.

She had never been in a situation where she was the only one of her kind in a place. She felt strange and uncomfortable. Aiden looked at her and he sensed that she was uncomfortable. So, he squeezed her hand. Amanda looked at him and he gave her a warm smile. They sat down and looked at their menus.

Amanda looked at her menu, but she couldn't read the writing. The words were odd little symbols she had never seen before. Aiden looked at her and saw her confusion.

"Oh, I'm sorry Amanda. You can't read Malatha yet. Let me help you."

He sat close to her and began reading the different names of the dishes for her. His breath was warm on Amanda's cheek and his scent was a masculine fragrance that smelled appealing to Amanda, and she tingled all over.

Abigail and Aaron were ready to order. Amanda made up her mind and she ordered the steak and shrimp platter. The waiter took their order. Amanda liked the restaurant. The lights were dim, the tables were square with beige tablecloths. There was a picture on the wall, a man in a boat with a net catching fish. There were candles on the table illuminating a soft white glow. Aiden reached for Amanda's hand and she eagerly put her hand in his, and she felt warm all over.

CHAPTER

7

Barnabas Drapers was in the engine room of his ship taking diagnostics of his engine. He had a mid-size cargo ship that he used to haul exports to Tanner Three, a planet in the Beta Quadrant. He had heard the news buzzing around town about the Earth women that the military had captured and brought to Malatha.

For the past two weeks, all he heard was how life was going to be better for the Malatha men now that they had new female companionship. He had no opinion about the ordinance that was passed concerning the women and he had no interest in obtaining one of his own.

His life was fine. He could come and go as he pleases. He didn't need any female clinging to him, and he definitely didn't need any children. He read the result on the computer screen. His engine was working at thirty percent. He needed a new plasma pistol. It was going to take several weeks for him to get it because he had to get it custom-made. That old engine was hitting his wallet hard.

He needed money and he needed it fast. His old gig was good hauling junk, but he needed something that will put him over the top. He needed something that will make him rich quick and easy. He thought about the cargo ship at the shipyard. It had his name on it. He could make his trip to the Beta Quadrant in twice the time in that new ship.

But how was he going to come up with that kind cash? He needed real cash. Then it hit him. It was the perfect plan. He grinned and patted his chest, proud of himself. It was a little dangerous and it could cost him his life, but it will be quick cash if he does it right.

He turned off his computer, wiped his hand on a towel, and went to the bridge of the ship. Cyr and Drogo were running diagnostics on the ship's computer when Barnabas came on the bridge.

"I've got an idea, fellows. It will make us some quick cash. It might even make us rich," Barnabas said smiling.

"Oh yeah, what is it?" Drogo asked, a little doubtful.

"You heard about those women Prime Minister Raincourt had brought here to be our new citizens?"

"Yeah, what about them?" asked Cyr.

"You know Cyprus Five in the Beta Quadrant? They have that sex slave operation going on. They are always looking for more women, and humanoid women are in high demand. Let's say we round up as many as we can and take them to Cyprus and sell them into slavery."

"That sounds good, but how are we going to do that? Those women are under tight security. But, I think it will be easy to break in the treasury department," Cyr said.

"No, I say we wait until they are free to come and go as they please. Then we take them," Barnabas said.

"But if we kidnapped them, they will be looking for us. We will be felons. They would put a universal warrant out for our arrest. We will be fugitives," Drogo said.

Barnabas thought for a second and then he smiled.

"What if we get them to go with us willingly and then no one will be looking for them?" Barnabas said smiling.

"But the women who will be free would be the married ones. And others are going to stay in that compound. And the married ones, husbands will be looking for them!" Drogo protested.

"But when they notice, we will be long gone. Come on Drogo! This is a good idea. My best plan ever! We can't get caught. I'm telling you it's going to work. We don't need that many women. Let's say about twenty-five or thirty."

"And then how are we going to get them to Cyprus Five?" Cyr asked.

"In this ship," Barnabas answered.

"We can't even go to the moon on this ship," Drogo said.

"I'm saying when we fix the engine. All we need to do is get to Cyprus Five. Once we get there, we can buy a new ship."

"I don't know. We can get in a lot of trouble," Drogo said.

"Come on, man. What are you a man or a mouse?"

"I'm a man, but I want to be a free man, not one behind bars or sentenced for life to freeze to death in the cold planet of Creeley."

"We won't get into any trouble. Have I ever let you down before?" Barnabas asked Drogo.

"No," Drogo answered.

"Ever since mom died, I've always had your back. Haven't I?" Barnabas asked Drogo.

"Yes," Drogo answered.

"Well, I'm not going to let anything happen to you now. You are my little brother and I promise mom that I would look out for you. Well, am I not doing that?"

"Yes," Drogo said, feeling a little uneasy. He wanted to get a wife of his own. But now, he's going to be on the run with Barnabas and Cyr.

"This is a good plan. It has to work. I'm putting my ship on it and you know how much I love this old thing," Barnabas said grinning.

"I was reading the news the other day. Chancellor De Ivory is going to have a worldwide lottery on Monday. Pretty soon the streets would be filled with Earth women. All we have to do is talk to some of them into going with us. What do you know about those women Cyr?"

"Well, I heard that they were taken from their home planet Earth. So, some of them would want to go back home."

"That's interesting. We can go with that. We would tell them we would take them back home if they go with us."

"But why would they want to believe you? They would know you want something in return," Drogo retorted.

"I see what you're saying, Drogo. What else do you know about them?"

"I don't know."

"I heard that they are very religious," Cyr said.

"That's good! We could tell them that we are missionaries, and it's our calling to right the wrong our government has done. They will believe us!" "What if we get caught?" Drogo asked.

"We won't get caught. We will be careful. We will be selective with who we try to persuade to go with us. We would tell the girls not to tell anyone, especially not their husband. This will work! It's the perfect plan! All we need is about twenty or thirty humanoid girls and we will be rich. So, are you in Drogo?"

Drogo thought for a while. He knew that this was a foolish plan, one of Barnabas' most daring yet, but Barnabas had done a lot for him especially after their mother died. And he was his brother. He didn't want to let him down. Maybe it will work. It had to.

"Alright, I'm in," he finally said.

"That's my little brother talking! You will see we are going to be rich. Let's get all of the info that we can on these women and learn everything that we can. I have to make a call."

Barnabas went into his office and sat down at his desk. He brought up his call screen and called Tobias. An image came up on the screen. It was Tobias, a short stout man who served on the mission to Earth. He was a cook in the dining lounge in Section C655.

"What can I do for you Barnabas?" he asked, disgusted.

"Tobias, you know that favor you owe me?"

Tobias hesitated. "Yes."

"Well I'm calling to cash in," Barnabas grinned.

"What do you want?" Tobias asked, a little frightened that Barnabas was going to ask for something big.

"I need you to get all the information you can get on those Earth women and give it to me."

"What? Why?" Tobias asked. "They are nothing but some poor old women that the military brought here." "I want all the info you can give me." "Why?" Tobias asked again.

"Because I have an idea to make a little cash. I'm going to round up as many as I can and sell them into sex slavery on Cyprus Five."

Tobias' mouth dropped to the ground. He was stunned. He knew Barnabas was a snake, but he didn't know he would stoop this low.

"Do you know the penalty for harming those women? It's death. I don't want to be a part of this!"

"You won't be involved. If we get caught, I won't mention your name. I'll take the heat on my own, but it's a good idea. I'm sure we won't get caught."

"Who are all in it with you?" Tobias asked.

"It's just me, Drogo, my brother, and my old pal Cyr."

Tobias knew that Cyr was a snake like Barnabas, but Drogo was too young. Barnabas was going to drag him down with them.

"Okay, Barnabas. I'll download for you the information and send it to your computer. After that, I don't owe you anything anymore." "Your slate is clean, Tobias," Barnabas laughed.

CHAPTER

Aiden took Amanda to their rooms. It was a bedroom with another room adjacent to it. The rooms were large it was like having their own apartment. The bed was along the left wall. It was a big king-size bed with a metallic-colored comforter set and lots of pillows. A dresser with an attached mirror was across the bed. There was a nightstand on both sides of the bed and a tall chest of drawers near the walk-in closet.

The adjacent room was made of glass and it had a pretty silver furniture set and a chest in front of the couch. Some papers that looked like music sheets were on top of the chest. There was a strange-looking stringed instrument that looked like a guitar sitting in the corner by a silver chair.

Amanda liked the rooms. She felt comfortable and safe; she felt at home. Her room in Chicago could fit in that room five times. She could see the garden in the backyard by just looking out the glass walls. She felt welcome. She knew that Aiden was trying everything in his power to please her, but she just wanted to see her grandmother and Steve one last time.

Amanda walked over to the bed and looked down at it. She then looked at Aiden.

"This is beautiful, Aiden. The rooms are nice, I love it very much, but where are you going to sleep?" she asked.

Aiden's jaw dropped. He looked at Amanda for a long while.

"I'm going to sleep here with you," he finally said. "We are married now. There is nothing wrong with it. We are together."

Amanda's heart jumped to her throat. She had never been with any boy before. She wasn't ready for this. Everything was going too fast. What was she going to do? She had to think of something quick before evening.

"Tomorrow, we can go shopping and get you some clothes," Aiden said smiling.

He then turned and walked out of the door. Aiden walked downstairs and into the parlor. He looked out of the double glass doors, at his mother sitting by the pool. His heart was heavy because he knew that Amanda wasn't happy.

He knew she was just going through the motions because she had no other choice.

"Chancellor De Ivory made her come with me," he thought. "I want Amanda to fall in love with me and love me. I want her to forget about her old family. I'm her family now. What can I do to make her see that everything is going to be all right? I don't want to force her or scare her into loving me. I want everything to be natural. I want her to love me with her whole heart. I love her. I loved her from the moment I saw her, and I know she loves me. She's just afraid to let go."

He looked out into the yard at the birds flying around the flowers. They look so happy with no care in the world. How come people can't be like that? "We have to worry about everything," he thought. He looked at his mother sitting by the pool and he thought about his parents' marriage and how they spent their lives together. His father was lucky he was one of the few men on Malatha who had a wife. They were together for over thirty years.

His parents still love and respect one another. That's what he wants with Amanda. He wants that same love and respect his father had. "I'll talk to mom. She'll know what to do," he said as he walked out of the door.

Abigail was reading a magazine as she sat by the pool, which she likes to do on warm slow days. It was quiet and the sun was shining warmly on her face, giving her a bronze glow. She was in complete solitude. The yard was big and spacious, so, she didn't have to worry about her neighbors.

Although she does have neighbors on both sides, they were too far away to bother her.

She had the privilege of the country but lived in the city. She was looking at an ad in the magazine, an image of a man and woman walking along the beach, hand in hand while the tides rolled in. It was a perfume ad and it gave Abigail an idea for a painting. She thought that she might start on it tomorrow. She loved it when inspiration hit her suddenly.

She liked spontaneity; it fueled her passion for painting. Abigail was an artist and a very talented one. She sold her paintings in art galleries all around Malatha. She had met Aaron in undergraduate school and they got married right after graduation. Aaron had a good job as an aerospace engineer and that gave Abigail a chance to work as an artist.

She thought that Aiden was going to be an artist too. He had the talent for it, but he took after his father and joined the military and it paid off. He has seen a great deal of the galaxy and he has seen some combat as well. She hoped he would settle down and get a civilian job when Amanda gets pregnant, Abigail thought.

"My nerves can't take it when he is deployed so far away. Aaron settled down when Aiden was born, and his civilian life had made us a good living. I hope Aiden does the same. I don't want to get that call one day," an intense sensation moved through her as she shivered at the thought.

"But the military has been good to Aiden and he's up for a promotion," she said trying to put the bad thoughts out of her mind. "He's been out of infantry for two years now."

"He loves being, Col. Galveston's assistant," she continued. "I'll just sleep better at night knowing he's safe and sound at home. Amanda is a good girl. She will make an excellent wife when she gets used to being here. I sense that she likes Aiden. And he really likes her. I have always wondered what it would be like to see Aiden in love. It's beautiful my son is growing up. I thought this day would never come. Pretty soon this house will be full of children. I could teach them to draw and paint and I can teach my granddaughter to cook," Abigail said to herself.

Aiden walked up to Abigail.

"Mom."

Abigail looked up from her magazine.

"I showed Amanda the rooms. She really liked them. She thought that they were beautiful. You did a good job decorating. Thank you mom, but –," Aiden hesitated.

"But what? Aiden what's wrong?" Abigail asked as she looked at him. She knew when something bothered her son. He would look at her with his big round brown eyes.

"It's nothing. Maybe it's all in my mind."

"What's on your mind?" Abigail asked, concerned for him.

"I sense a little anxiousness in Amanda. A part of her is closed off from me. I tried to talk to her and let her know everything is going to be okay, but she is still nervous. I don't know what to do." "I see," Abigail said.

"You think she is still anxious from what has happened to her?" Abigail asked.

"Yes," Aiden answered in a low voice.

"Just give her a little time. What you should do is take her out. Show her a good time. Take her to Jin's place. She will like that. There are a lot of things to do there and all the young men hang out there. She has to see that Malatha is no different than Earth. I sense her nervousness too, Aiden. But all we could do is make her comfortable."

"I also know that she really likes you. You just have to give her a little time. Don't get discouraged. You just brought her here today. Things aren't going to happen overnight. Just talk to her. You have to be her friend and try to understand her feelings. That's the only way that this is going to work.

CHAPTER

Chancellor De Ivory was busy all week matching the men with the women from Earth. He had paired up all of the military men and now he was working on the civilians. He matched each man with a woman in his age group. To be fair, he held a lottery because it was the easiest and fairest way to make the matches without bias.

The women had begun to feel at home, and they were cooperating fully. They looked forward to being matched with a mate. The men were happy with their selection and there were no complaints. The women had begun to go about their lives as normal citizens of Malatha.

The shops, restaurants, and businesses were full of them. Gaul and the other continents had begun to look like a full-functioning society. The women started to adapt to Malatha traditions and culture as if it was their own.

They had no anger or animosity toward the Malatha people who brought them there. In fact, some of the women believed that they were better off on Malatha than in the United States. Chancellor De Ivory appointed two Earth women from every continent to be ambassadors.

If the women had a complaint or concern, they would relay it to the ambassadors and the ambassadors will relay the matter to Chancellor De Ivory. The ambassadors would also inform the chancellor of the goods and services needed by the women. Chancellor De Ivory had relayed the information to the Department of Commerce. Businesses offering the goods and services moved in a hurry to provide for them.

One of the concerns of the women was how to earn their own money and hold a position. Chancellor De Ivory took the matter up to the prime minister and his cabinet. They were to hold a meeting on Friday morning concerning the matter.

Chancellor De Ivory wanted Diana Johnson, one of the ambassadors he appointed, to attend the meeting because she was very intelligent and was a congresswoman on Earth. She spoke very well too. Chancellor De Ivory told her to write down all of the concerns of the women so she could present them to the prime minister.

The chancellor wrote his report thoroughly about the matching of couples. One of the concerns of the cabinet was that they didn't want any problem with the men wanting the same woman.

Chancellor De Ivory wrote that his method was fair and without bias and the men seemed happy. The other concern was about the women who needed infusement treatment. Chancellor De Ivory wrote that the treatment was going well, that there were no deaths, and that the women seemed to respond to the treatment well.

The day of the meeting came and Prime Minister Raincourt, together with his cabinet, had entered the conference hall. It was a large room that had a long oval table and ten leather chairs around it. Prime Minister Raincourt sat at the head and Chancellor De Ivory on the other end. The cabinet members gathered around the table.

"Did the men understand that the women were to be their equal partners in a relationship and not their property?" Prime Minister Raincourt asked.

"Yes, it was written in their contract, was read and explained to each of them before they signed it. The men understood that the women were human beings to be treated with dignity and respect. They also knew the penalty of harming the women or mistreating them," Chancellor De Ivory answered.

"The women know that they are to behave like wives and helpmates to their husbands and act in a manner that would not bring shame to their husbands," Chancellor De Ivory stated.

The chancellor brought in Diana Johnson and she read her report. Prime Minister Raincourt was impressed at how well she presented herself before the cabinet. They thanked her and told her how well she did.

Then Chancellor De Ivory told her to wait for him in his chambers. Diana left and the cabinet talked over the matter. The members debated on the matter and Prime Minister Raincourt decided that the women should be able to attend school and hold minimal jobs, but to hold a position of authority or in government was out of the question.

However, their offspring could because they will be sons and daughters of Malatha men. Chancellor De Ivory brought up the matter of voting, which is the right of every Malatha citizen. Prime Minister Raincourt and the cabinet members debated on the issue as well.

"The women shouldn't have the right to vote because they are not Malatha-born and only know little about our way of life. It will make things unbalanced," Edward D'Ambray stated.

"The women should be treated like Malatha citizens. They should be able to vote. If you take that right from them, they will become secondclass citizens," Col. Galveston said.

Raincourt listened to both sides of the issue and after thinking about the matter, he stated,

"The women should have the right to vote, but they could only vote in the party that their husbands affiliated with. They can't change parties on their own."

Everyone agreed. The chancellor brought up the matter of divorce.

"An Earth woman cannot divorce her husband no matter what the circumstances, and similarly, Malatha men cannot divorce his wife unless she is proven to be unable to adapt to the ways of Malatha society and that has to be proven as well," Raincourt stated.

Chancellor De Ivory brought up the concern of space travel. The whole cabinet was in agreement.

"Under no circumstances could an Earth woman leave Malatha, not even to go to Dacia. If any man has family on Dacia, he could take his offspring, but not his wife, but she could travel throughout the continents of Malatha," Raincourt said.

"Are there any other concerns?" Prime Minister Raincourt asked.

"None at the moment," Chancellor De Ivory replied.

Raincourt adjourned the meeting and De Ivory went back to his chambers. He told Diana Johnson that she did well. Now he had to go write up the laws and post them so that the new Malatha couples could see them.

He had also planned to discuss the new law in adjustment training with the women. He felt that all the laws were fair. It gave the women some freedom but not enough to take over society. He looked forward to discussing it in the upcoming weeks with the women.

CHAPTER

10

Aiden took Amanda for a ride in his new two-door red convertible sports hovercar. Amanda's eyes sparkled and she grinned from ear to ear. This was Aiden's prized possession which he bought a year ago on Dacia after he got his promotion to First Lieutenant.

He had only driven it once before he was deployed to Earth. He thought he would take a drive to the city to show Amanda around, but first, he took a detour through the countryside. Amanda loved the scenery of the country. She loved the green grass and the trees. She liked the occasional houses she saw along the road.

The air was fresh and clean and the smell of the flowers marched up Amanda's nose, putting her in a good mood. She enjoyed being with Aiden. He was so gentle with her. She could see his affection. She was beginning to feel safe.

He looked at her with his big brown eyes and her heart melted. She wanted to hug and kiss him as a warm sensation went through her body like a rushing wave going to shore.

"Stop this Amanda," she thought. "You must not forget."

She turned her head and looked out the countryside, but that warm feeling stayed and kept tingling her body parts. Amanda was in love and that made her angry.

Aiden looked at Amanda. He could see the affection for him in her eyes, no matter how hard she tried to close herself off. He tried harder to win her affection. He knew that Amanda enjoyed riding through the country. She enjoyed being here, but she was still afraid to show her emotions. Still, he would continue to be loving and gentle until she breaks her walls down completely and give in.

If this is a game she was playing, he was determined to win it. He put the car in gear and sped down the road. The car could go up to seven hundred miles per hour in thirty seconds. There were no other cars on the road. So, Aiden ramped up the speed.

"Hold on," he said as the car geared up.

Amanda screamed with excitement as the car flew down the road. She grabbed Aiden by the arm. She had never been in anything so fast. But, she wasn't afraid. She enjoyed the thrill of speeding down the road. Aiden slowed down and Amanda laughed out loud it was a warm hearty laugh.

Aiden enjoyed hearing her laugh.

"You enjoyed that Amanda?" he asked.

Amanda grinned.

"I know a little spot just down the road. I go there when I want to be alone. I think you will enjoy it."

He drove down the road and Amanda looked out at the countryside.

He finally stopped and parked the car then he and Amanda got out. They walked through a cluster of trees to a crystal blue lake. The lake was beautiful, so were the surrounding land and trees. There was a bench sitting near the lake and Amanda and Aiden sat down.

Amanda's eyes gleamed and she smiled gently at Aiden.

"This is so beautiful Aiden. I never got to the chance to see anything like this at home. I've always wanted to visit the country, but I never got the chance. I had to work to help my family and study. We weren't rich people. I had to work at a young age to help my grandmother."

"I understand," Aiden said. "Now you can come here, whenever you like. You don't have to worry about anything, because I'm here. Let me love you Amanda and you would see. You will have a good life, an easy life. Not like what you had on earth, but a better life." He looked at Amanda's eyes and her heart leaped.

Aiden is sincere, she thought.

"I can love him and let go. He's a strong, handsome, and smart man. He will protect me here in this strange beautiful land. I should let go and fall in love," Amanda thought.

Aiden leaned over and kissed her, and a tingling sensation went through her body and her head began to spin. Amanda's lips were soft and full, and Aiden didn't want to stop kissing her. A warm feeling went through him and stabbed at his heart.

"Amanda is quiet. She didn't talk too much. But I won't get tired of her chatter either. She is pretty and smart. I do love her," he thought.

Aiden looked into Amanda's eyes and she felt a warm glow flow through her. Aiden could see the satisfaction in her eyes. Amanda was blissfully happy. She had lost all her will to resist. Her heart sang with delight.

Aiden could feel her affection for him and he was pleased with himself. He put his arm around Amanda, and she laid her head on his shoulder.

"I have never been with a guy before," she said in a low voice. "This is new to me."

Aiden listened, pleased that he was her first one.

"Don't be afraid, Amanda. I won't hurt you. You are safe here. I love you. You are a part of my family now," Aiden said.

A cool breeze blew across Amanda's face and she welcomed it. It cooled off the warm sensation in her heart. As much as she hated to admit it, she loved Aiden too. She tried hard to remember her grandmother, but for now, she couldn't remember what she looked like.

Aiden stood up, picked a stone, and threw it into the lake. The stone skipped across the lake, making ripples in the water. Amanda raised her hand to her mouth and giggled.

"Do you want to try?" Aiden said handing her a stone.

Amanda threw the stone, but it sank to the bottom. Aiden laughed a thunderous laugh.

"No, silly," he said.

He stood behind her, took her arm, and gently flicked her wrist. The stone skipped across the lake.

Amanda melted in Aiden's arms. Aiden's nose rested on Amanda's head and he smelled her freshly cleaned hair and his heart sang with affection. "This is my favorite spot too, Aiden," Amanda said smiling at Aiden. "We can come here together when you want to get away," she continued.

"Okay," Aiden said smiling.

"I love it here. I really do," Amanda said jumping up and down.

Aiden was amused at Amanda's excitement. She was like a child receiving a gift.

"Are you hungry?" he asked.

"Let's go grab a bite to eat."

They walked back to the car hand in hand. They walked through the woods and the cluster of trees.

Amanda turned around and looked at the lake one last time before she got in the car.

CHAPTER

Aiden loved Jin's place. It was a little nightspot where all the soldiers hung out while they were on leave. It had live music and a dance floor.

Aiden would come here to unwind after work. He found a table in the back near the stage and he and Amanda sat down.

Aiden order two beers. Amanda didn't drink beer, but she was curious to try it. The waiter brought two large mugs of a green foamy substance and Amanda's eyes widened. Aiden took a sip first then Amanda tasted it.

It was cool and tart-like, just like root beer. So, Amanda took a huge swallow.

"Are you hungry?" Aiden asked handing her a menu.

"You order for me. I trust you Aiden," Amanda said.

"Let's see, do you like this? What do they call it on your planet?

"Roast beef?"

"Well, this is like roast beef with cheese, lettuce, and tomato. It's really big, you probably can't eat it all."

"I'll have that," Amanda said.

Aiden smiled and called the waiter. Amanda is beginning to trust him. That's a good sign, he thought.

The waiter came and took their order and brought them two more beers. Amanda really liked the beer. It was cool and satisfying. Just something she needs, because she was out in the hot sun.

She looked around and noticed that other black women were in the bar with their husbands. She didn't stick out like a sore thumb anymore.

"So, what did you do for fun in your spare time on Earth?" Aiden asked.

Amanda thought for a moment then she smiled.

"Well, I used to go to my school's football games. My school would have a dance every Friday night for the juniors and seniors. They were a lot of fun. We got to dress up and dance 'til midnight. My friends used to throw house parties and I would go and dance and listen to music." "So, you like to dance?" Aiden asked smiling.

"Yes, I use to dance a lot. I'm a good dancer. I like sports too. I like basketball and football." Aiden smiled.

"We have sports here too! I like wrestling. It's a big deal around here. Lightning Bolt The Crusher is my favorite. He is undefeated. He is big and mean. You would like him. When he comes to town, I'll take you to a match. We have other sports, but they are too hard to explain. I'll show you on the viewing screen."

"Well, do you like movies?" he asked.

"Yes, I love movies!" Amanda answered excitedly.

"We have movie theaters, playhouses, and orchestras. I like romance movies," Amanda said laughing.

"We have romance. We have horror too. I like action movies that involve bad guys and law enforcement," Aiden said.

Men with strange instruments came on stage. Aiden clapped and whistled as a tall man wearing funny clothes walked up to a mic.

"How are you doing Jin's place?" he said.

All the men cheered.

"We are going to play a dance number for you to get things warmed up. I see we have our new female citizens here tonight. Give them a round of applause!"

The men clapped and cheered and the band began to play. Amanda was amused because the music sounded like a mixture of big band swing music and heavy metal. It was loud and fast.

Aiden took Amanda by the hand.

"Do you want to dance?" he asked as he pulled her to the dance floor.

Amanda's heart raced. She didn't know how to move to that kind of music. Aiden began dancing first. He started hopping from side to side, from one foot to the other, moving his arms in a wavy motion.

Amanda was surprised he was actually moving to the music.

So, she mocked him. Other couples got up to dance. The dance floor got crowded. Amanda let go of her distrusts and a feeling of joy came over her. She wanted to dance all night. When the song ended, they went back to their table.

Aiden looked up and saw his friends from work, Bartholomew, Milo, and Basil, coming through the door. They had their wives with them.

"Bartholomew!" Aiden called.

Bartholomew looked at him and waved. They went over to Aiden's table. "Hey, brothers," Aiden said as he shook their hands.

Milo grabbed a table and pulled it over to Aiden's. They all sat down.

"These are our wives," Bartholomew said.

"This is Holly, my wife. Grace, Basil's wife. And Donna, Milo's wife. How long have you been here?" Bartholomew asked.

"Not too long. About an hour," Aiden answered.

Amanda looked at the way Holly, Grace, and Donna held onto their alien mates. It was like they were really in love. The music was playing, and they were really having a good time. Amanda looked around the whole bar and all the women were having a good time.

"Is it me or is everyone happy with what's going on?" she thought.

Holly grabbed Bartholomew by the hand, and he squeezed it. So, Amanda grabbed Aiden by the hand and giggled.

"Have you ordered yet?" Milo asked.

"Yes, it's really busy tonight, so they are pretty slow." Bartholomew called for the waiter.

"They are issuing military housing on the Twenty-Second at Green View Street. We signed up for one. You should too Aiden, and then we could be neighbors," Basil said.

"I know. I've been thinking about it, but I decided not just yet. My parents prepared some rooms for us in their house. They'll be disappointed if I suddenly move."

"Do you know the military is giving us all kinds of incentives for taking a wife?" Bartholomew asked.

"I know and I'm taking advantage of them, but not the housing just yet."

"Did you read the new laws concerning the women that Chancellor De Ivory posted?" Milo asked.

"Yes, I was going to talk to Amanda about it tomorrow." Amanda looked at Aiden frightened.

"It's nothing to worry about," he said to her trying to reassure her, as he squeezed her hand.

The waiter came over to take their order.

"Your order is coming up," he said to Aiden.

"Could you hold our order until their orders are ready?" Aiden asked.

"Okay," the waiter answered, and he went back to the kitchen. The band began to play again.

"Let's dance!" Holly shouted.

She grabbed Bartholomew by the arm. He grinned and stood up and they went to the dance floor. Milo and Basil followed. Amanda smiled.

"Do you want to dance?" she asked.

Aiden grabbed her and pulled her to the dance floor. The band played a slow number and Aiden grabbed Amanda by the waist, pulling her close. Amanda closed her eyes and swayed to the music.

"Holly and Grace are really having a good time. Don't they care about what has happened to them?" she thought as she looked over at them. Aiden pulled her close and she moved to the music, trying to forget everything that happened.

CHAPTER

12

The coffee shop was crowded when Col. Galveston and his wife Chantel Lee walked in. Chantel's heart jolted and a warm sensation moved through her as she looked at Galveston. Of all the women, she was the one chosen to be his wife. Col. Galveston was happy with his choice. Chantel was beautiful, tall, dark, and slim. She had a full oval face and long hair, and she was smart.

She taught high school math on Earth. They sat down at a table by the window. Galveston called for the waiter.

"When you complete your adjustment training you could probably teach school here," he said smiling.

Chancellor De Ivory allowed her to assist him in teaching the women about the culture and way of life on Malatha. De Ivory praised her highly when Col. Galveston chose her.

"We are having a dinner party to introduce you to my colleagues. That will be a good opportunity for you to get to know everyone," he continued. "I was thinking we will start having children early. I want my first son to attend the Military Academy on Dacia."

Chantel's eyes widened as she wasn't sure if she could have children. She tried on Earth, but without success. She knew that medicine was advanced on Malatha, but she didn't know if they had methods for fertility. She was already thirty years old and she had been trying for two years to get pregnant.

She bit her bottom lip and waves moved through her stomach.

"Should I tell him?" she thought. She didn't want to disappoint him. Maybe she should tell him, so he could choose someone else. She listened as Col. Galveston went on and on about his future son.

"Our house is large and it has plenty of room for a large family," he continued. "I thought the room overlooking the backyard would be a little girl's room. It's the one down the hall from the master."

Chantel nodded her head yes. "Maybe I should tell him. I don't want to disappoint him. I don't want to start our relationship off being deceitful," Col. Galveston looked at Chantel and saw that she was a million miles away.

"Is there anything wrong?" he asked, interrupting her thoughts.

She looked at him and smiled.

"Bardolph," she said as she put her hand on his hand.

"I'm thirty already. I tried for two years on Earth to get pregnant, but every attempt failed."

"Did you go to the doctor? They have methods on Earth to help you conceive."

"No, I didn't have that kind of money on a teacher's salary."

Col. Galveston laughed.

"Your medical exams say you are fine. If we can't conceive the oldfashioned way, we will seek a doctor. The medicine here is more advanced than on Earth. We can make you conceive even way into your seventies. We did it before with Malatha women. We can do it with you. Don't worry. That's why we asked for women from infant to sixty."

Chantel's pulse slowed down and she breathed a sigh of relief. The waiter came to take their order.

"I would like two of your strong mountain blend," Col. Galveston said. "And two tart pastries please," he said as he grabbed Chantel by the hand and leaned forward to kiss her.

Chantel's heart skipped a beat and her head began to spin. Galveston was gentle and caring. She had forgotten about her boyfriend on Earth with whom she was engaged to be married, but she was taken to come to Malatha. She was happy when Chancellor De Ivory told her that she was chosen for a mate.

She thought that she would die if she spent one more day at the compound. The waiter brought the coffee and pastry. Chantel tasted her coffee – it was strong and bitter, just like she liked it. The pastry was sweet and flaky.

She wasn't sure what kind of fruit was in the pastry, but it didn't overwhelm the flavor. She was amazed at how much Malatha was similar to Earth in many ways.

She thought she might try that new recipe that Chancellor De Ivory taught the women to make in adjustment training. She liked to try new things. Her reading and writing were coming along well too. She could read her menu and the news posts.

"Can you buy me a Malatha cookbook?" she asked Col. Galveston. He looked at her.

"Yes, I can get you a cookbook. My mother has lots of our family recipes. She would love to share them with you," he said smiling.

"That's great," Chantel said excitedly.

"I love to cook and make things. I could cook some recipes from Earth for you," she said.

"That sounds great! I would love that," Col. Galveston said.

"This pastry is good," she said.

"It's made from a berry they grow here on Malatha. One day I am going to take you to the country to show you how the vegetation grows here on Malatha."

"I would like to go to Dacia," she said. Col. Galveston's heart dropped.

"We talked about that. You can't leave Malatha, but if you want we could take a cruise to Parthia. It's mostly wilderness but you will love it," he said.

Chantel smiled and took another sip of her coffee.

The sun was large and high in the sky, illuminating a yellowish glow on the beach. The ocean was a dazzling blue that stretched as far as the eye could see. Amanda ran barefoot into the water, meeting the tide as it came rolling to shore. She had never been so happy. She always wanted to go to the beach. A real beach. Not like the beaches in Chicago, but a real beach near the ocean.

The water was warm on her toes as she ran along the shore.

"It's beautiful here!" she yelled out to Aiden, who was sitting on a blanket on the sand watching her.

"Amanda seems happy now. Maybe mom was right. I needed to spend more time with her," he thought.

Amanda danced around, running in and out of the water as the tide came rolling in. She looked off into the distance and saw a ship. It looked like a cruise ship or a passenger ship of some kind.

"Where could that ship be going? What's on the other side of this ocean?" she thought.

She turned and looked at Aiden, who had laid back on his elbows.

"He seems happy. Maybe this could work. We have the same interest," Amanda thought. She reached down and picked up a speckled brown seashell. It was the first time she had ever seen one. She ran over to show Aiden.

Aiden sat up and looked at the shell.

"You put it up to your ears and you could hear the ocean," he said.

Amanda put the shell up to her ears. The shell made a humming sound in her ears. She sat down next to Aiden and looked out into the ocean.

"When I was a little girl, before my grandfather died, he would take me to the lagoon at the park. I used to imagine that I was in Florida or a lake, or some exotic place overseas, fishing."

"I used to go to the library and read magazines about traveling to places like France or Italy. I would collect those magazines and read them over and over. I made a list of things I was going to do when I graduate college and going to see the ocean was at the top of my list. I was going to take my grandmother and Steve away from that neighborhood. I had prayed all of my life that God would make me able."

"When they came to take me, I thought my life was over, but I see it is just beginning. I love it here Aiden. This is really a beautiful place. Thank you for bringing me here," she said.

Aiden looked at Amanda and his heart went out for her. He saw that she was vulnerable, and he wanted to rid her of all of her pain of losing her family.

He put his arm around her, and they sat and watched the tide.

"I wanted to take you here Amanda. This place means a lot to me. My father used to take me here when I was a little boy. He used to show me how to fight and handle my weapons. So, when I went to the military academy I would be prepared. This is just one of the beaches in Gaul and this one is small. There are some large beaches more spectacular than this."

"When I first went into the military, I was deployed on parent a planet in the Beta Quadrant and it had some nice beaches. The sand was a deep dark red and the ocean was gray. The planet had two moons and when you looked up in the sky, you could see the two moons at the same time. One of the moons was very large and closer than the other one. It was like you could reach out and touch it. The atmosphere on that planet was cold. It was cold year-round and the nights were long, and the days were short. In some areas of the planet, it stayed dark all the time. The moon didn't even shine there. It was thick dark, a strange kind of dark. Without any kind of light, you couldn't even see your hand if you put it up in front of your face! I was there because Malatha put a military outpost there. I stayed there for two long years."

"I wish I could go there," Amanda said.

"It wasn't a vacation spot for tours. It was harsh, cold, and desolate. You wouldn't like it. One day I am going to take you to Lanshire. It has large white sandy beaches and clear blue waters. It has a lot of wildlife there.

One of our oldest zoos is located there. Have you ever been to the zoo?"

"Yes," Amanda laughed. "Chicago has two zoos. I've been to both."

"Do you know how to swim? We could go swimming under the water and look at the coral reefs and tropical fish." "I would love that," Amanda said.

Aiden put his arm around her, pulled her close, and kissed her. Amanda melted in his arms as she eagerly kissed him back.

"Aiden is a gentleman even though he isn't human. He still has values like honesty and respect. These are the things I want in a man," Amanda thought.

She felt safe around Aiden, but she fought hard to remember her grandmother and Steve. She was not going to forget. Someday, somehow, she was going to find out how to get back home. A tingling sensation moved through Aiden as he kissed Amanda. He was falling deeper and deeper in love and he hoped that Amanda was too.

CHAPTER

13

Hope was admiring the dresses in the window of the shop at the shopping center. The shopping district was a busy large place full of people looking for bargains. It stretched for ten city blocks. Hope was chosen to marry a doctor who was slightly older than she was, but he was a kind and gentle man who gave her the freedom to come and go as she pleases.

Their house was large and old. A brick and wood house with a long porch wiped around it. It reminded Hope of an old farmhouse on Earth. It was beautiful, but it was nothing like she had on Earth. Her only job was to keep it maintained.

Ingram LeBlanc had a private practice in a building adjacent to the house. So, he was always at home. He had taken Hope to the shopping center twice before and while she was there, she had ordered a specially made dress. It was ready to be picked up that day.

Dr. LeBlanc was busy with a streak of patients. So, he allowed Hope to go to the shopping center on her own. She caught a cab, which picked her up in front of her house and drove her to the shopping center. She walked around several shops before going to the dress shop. She thought she might have a bite to eat after she picked up her dress.

She went into the shop and looked around at the dresses before going up to the counter to pick her dress up. She saw a pretty little lace dress with a matching lace scarf that she decided to try on. She took the dress off the rack and went into the dressing room.

When entering the dressing room, Faith Smith, a girl she met at the compound was coming out.

"Hope!" she called.

Hope looked around and smiled.

"Faith, what are you doing here?" she asked.

"I'm shopping for a dress. My husband is having a party tonight. I need something pretty to wear," she said.

"Oh," Hope said.

"What are you doing here?" Faith asked smiling.

"I had a dress made for me and I'm here to pick it up and then I saw this one and decided to try it on. So, how have you been doing?" Hope asked. "I haven't seen you since I left the compound," she continued.

"Well, after you got chosen, I stayed at the compound for a week. Then they chose me. My husband is a musician. He travels a lot, but when he's on Malatha I could travel with him. We are going to Parthia next month," Faith said, excited.

"That sounds good! My husband is a doctor. He has a small practice that he runs from home. He is always busy with patients. He lets me help him sometimes, but I really don't know much about medicine. He's nice though, I guess I like him," Hope said.

"Do you have time? Do you want to go grab a bite to eat?" Faith asked.

"Yes, just let me try on this dress," Hope said as she went into the dressing room.

She took off her clothes and tried on the lace dress. It was slim, hugging her hips the way she wanted it to.

"Ingram would love me in this," she said as she looked in the mirror.

She took it off, put it back on the hanger and stepped out from the dressing room. She went up to the checkout counter to buy the dress. Faith followed. Hope asked the clerk for the dress she had made. The clerk went to the back to get the dress. When she returned, she rung up the two dresses. Hope put her thumbprint on a purchase pad and the purchase went into Dr. LeBlanc's account. They walked out of the dress shop and down the street to a sandwich shop where Hope and her husband had dined at before. They found a table by the window so they could look out at the busy crowd of shoppers. Hope motioned for the waiter.

"So, do you live near here?" Faith asked smiling at Hope.

"I live a couple of miles away on a quiet tree-lined street near the beach," Hope said.

"The house is big and beautiful, but it's only me and Ingram. I guess he was pretty lonely before I came. He wants to fill the house up with children."

"Well, we live in a condo in the business district," Faith said. "I don't think my husband wants any children right now." The waiter came to take their order.

"I would like the Uralum sandwich and a cup of coffee," Hope said.

"And I'll try the Caba Sandwich and a beer," Faith said.

The waiter went into the back and placed their order.

Barnabas and Cyr were sitting at a table next to theirs. Barnabas looked at Faith and thought that she would be a good candidate for their plan. He got up and walked over to their table.

"Good afternoon ladies, my name is Barnabas. I run the mission downtown on Third and South. I, together with my congregation, was outraged at the inhumane way that the Malatha government brought you women to our planet."

"Slavery had been abolished on Malatha for thousands of years, but the way they brought you here is inhumane and is a form of slavery." Faith looked at him and shook her head in agreement.

"And did you know your own government sat back and allowed this to happen? This is disgraceful," Barnabas said looking at Hope and Faith, hoping he struck a chord.

"Would you like to sit down?" Hope said.

"Yes, thank you," he said. And so he sat down.

"My congregation and I have decided that we are not going to sit back and allow this iniquity to continue. Now, what I plan to do is gather as many of Malatha victims as I can and take them back to Earth." Hope looked at Barnabas.

"But it's against the law for us to leave the planet. We can't even space travel," she said.

"Now isn't that wrong? If you weren't slaves, you would have been free to come and go as you please. What I am saying is, I'm going to risk my life to take you safely home. Don't you want to see your friends and family?" "Yes," Faith said excitedly.

"Well, give me the honor to take you back. I feel that it's the calling that the Lord has directed me to do." He pulled out his tablet. "Now what are your names?" Hope got excited.

"My name is Hope."

"And my name is Faith."

They gave him their contact information. He wrote it all down on his tablet.

"Okay, Hope and Faith, you have two seats on my ship. I'll take you home. If you have any other women who would like to come along, give them my contact info and I will speak with them."

He gave them a card with his contact information on it.

"Don't tell anyone, especially your husbands. We wouldn't want to get in any trouble," he said as he stood up.

"I'll see you ladies later," he said as he walked out the door. Cyr followed close behind.

Abigail was in her workshop gathering paints and brushes and getting them ready to paint a portrait of Amanda. She thought that Amanda will make a good subject for one of her portraits. She had an easy face to look at, and Abigail could remember every detail of her face in her mind.

She noticed how Amanda had begun to open up to Aiden. For the past two weeks, they had been inseparable. Amanda was a nice quiet girl. She didn't give Abigail or Aaron any trouble. Since she had been there, Abigail hardly knew she was in the house.

Aiden was happier than usual. He's beginning to think that Amanda is starting to accept things as they are. Aiden is learning more and more about Amanda. Abigail thought as she envisioned both of them together.

"Pretty soon I would have a grandson or two," she said smiling, as she placed the canvas on her easel. "Malatha hasn't had any children in over twenty years. Aiden's generation were the last children. Now we will be a full-functioning and thriving race again," she said as she sat down to paint.

She imagined Amanda sitting in the tree swing in the backyard surrounded by flowers. The thought gave her a warm feeling inside. She liked Amanda and she had hoped that Amanda would love it here with them.

Throughout Aiden's life, he dreamed of getting married and when the government revealed their plans to take the Earth women, Aiden did research and learned everything he could about the African-American women, and he prepared himself for this day.

She thought as she began to paint.

"Now that he has chosen Amanda, he has been trying to win her affection, but I think she is coming around just nicely. Ever since she arrived, Amanda had been nothing but helpful to me. She helped with the household chores and with our dinner. I can imagine how nice it would have been to have a daughter. Now Amanda is beginning to be like a daughter to me," she thought as she smiled.

"I told Aiden that he had made an excellent choice. Amanda fit in just fine. Aaron liked her too. He thinks that she is a good mate for Aiden," she said as she thought of Aiden and Amanda together in their living room the first time Aiden brought her home.

Aiden opened up the door to his mother's workshop and peeked inside. Abigail turned around and smiled.

"I'm sorry mom. If you are busy I can come back later," he said.

Abigail looked at Aiden and noticed that he looked worried.

"Nonsense. I'm not busy son, come in," she said.

Aiden went in and closed the door. He walked up to her worktable and began fiddling with her brushes. Something was bothering him, Abigail thought. She knew when things bothered him. He behaved in that manner.

"What's wrong Aiden? Is there something wrong with Amanda?" Abigail asked, concerned.

"No, she is fine," Aiden said as he looked up at her.

"I have to go to work tomorrow and I don't want to leave Amanda here alone. She says she will be fine, but I don't trust her to be alone just yet. Could you keep an eye on her while I'm gone?"

"Just until I get used to leaving her alone."

Abigail looked at Aiden.

"Yes, I will watch out for her. She won't be alone. I'll be here all day."

"I know you will, but I need you to do more than just be here. I worried about this all night and it frightens me to think about it."

"Think about what Aiden?" Abigail asked as she began to get frightened.

"Could you just keep her from leaving the house by herself? I don't want her wandering off alone." Abigail's jaw dropped.

"I don't think she will wander off alone, but if you want me to keep her here, I will. I planned on going to the market tomorrow. I'll take her with me. She'll like that," Abigail said.

"Aiden a good relationship is based on trust. You have to trust Amanda. Keeping her hidden away in the house isn't good. One day she would have to go somewhere on her own."

Aiden's heart pounded as he listened to his mother. Her words pounded at his chest as he thought about what she said. Abigail looked at Aiden and it was a long while before he responded.

"I know, I just feel uneasy right now. I don't want anything to happen to her. Just do what I ask for a little while until she gets used to being here."

"I will, but Amanda is a good person. I don't think she is going to try to run away. Besides, where could she go? They would just bring her back. But don't worry I'll keep an eye on her until you get home from work."

"But Aiden, remember what I told you about trust. You have to learn to trust Amanda."

CHAPTER

14

The Malatha market was full of strange and exotic fruits and vegetables. Some of the fruits and vegetables looked similar to those on Earth.

Amanda looked at the almost impossible to pronounce names and chuckled. Her reading and writing were coming along fine in adjustment training, but she still had to get used to the strange alien sounds of the Malatha language.

Chancellor De Ivory said that the government was going to make English an alternative second language and she was thankful for that. She picked up a berry that was similar to a strawberry, but it was as big as her hand. In fact, all the fruits and vegetables were amazingly large compared to those on Earth.

The market was full of shoppers who were busy shopping for their evening supper. It was in the shopping center in the business district. The shopping center stretched for about two miles. You could buy anything you name there. Merchants from all over the planet traded there.

Amanda had never seen anything like it before. Abigail put something that looked like banana squash, but it was much larger in her cart. She got a couple of those large strawberries because she saw that Amanda admired them. She put a couple of more items in her cart.

Amanda put what looked like a grape, but it was as big as a half dollar, and she put it in her mouth. The fruit was filled with juice that was tartlike and sweet, much more than the grapes on Earth. A salesman was offering advertisements of some kind of sausage. They were long and round like the sausages from Earth.

He was cooking them in a skillet on an open flame. You could smell the spices and the aroma filled the room. It made Amanda hungry. He offered her a sample and she tasted it. It tasted like an Italian sausage but with a much stronger flavor, and it was also a bit spicy.

Abigail saw that Amanda liked it, so she put a couple of packages in her cart.

"This is an amazing place, Abigail. I have never been to a shopping center quite like this. We have malls in Chicago, and they are nice, but not quite like this," Amanda said.

"I'm glad you like it, Amanda. Maybe one day you can come here and shop for your family. There are other markets and shopping centers, but this is the largest. After we finish here, I'll take you to the dress shop and we can buy dresses for the weekend."

"Aaron is taking us to a play. Do you like plays Amanda?"

"Yes, I love plays. I've always wanted to go to New York and see a play on Broadway."

Abigail put a few more items in her basket.

"I think we have enough for tonight," she said as she went over to check out.

Amanda looked around and to her surprise, she saw Hope, her friend from the ship. She was looking at the giant strawberry. There was another girl with her whom Amanda didn't recognize.

"Excuse me Abigail, but I see my friend from the ship. I have to go and say hi," Amanda said pointing at Hope.

Abigail looked at Hope, then she thought about what Aiden had told her about looking out for Amanda. Hope looked harmless so she thought she'll let Amanda say hi.

"Okay, Amanda just for a few minutes. We have to go and get dinner done before the men get home."

"Okay," Amanda said as she walked over to Hope.

"Hope!" she called. Hope turned around.

"Amanda, I thought I'd never see you again," she said surprised.

They hugged and Amanda looked over her.

"You look well. I'm glad to see you," Amanda said.

"How have you been doing?" Amanda continued.

"I've been fine. This is Faith, a girl I met at the compound," Hope said.

Amanda looked at Faith and shook her hand.

"You are Amanda. Hope told me so much about you," Faith said smiling.

Hope told Amanda about her husband and her new house. Hope also told her how her husband trusted her to come and go as she pleases. Amanda told Hope about Aiden and his parents and her lack of freedom.

"I found a way to get home," Hope said excitedly.

Amanda was stunned. She didn't think that she heard Hope right.

"What did you say?" Amanda asked, straining to hear correctly.

"We have a way to get home back to Earth," Hope repeated.

"What? How?" Amanda asked surprised.

"Well, it's this missionary. He said that he was against what the Malatha government has done to us. So, he is going to take as many women as he can back to Earth."

Amanda took a deep breath and her heart began to pound.

"You believe him?" she asked.

"Yes," Hope said.

"I talked to him for a long time and he seems legitimate. But don't take my word for it. Call him and talk to him yourself and he would explain everything."

"When is he supposed to take you back?" Amanda asked.

"In about a month," Faith said.

"He needs to gather as many women as he can. He is risking everything to do this," she continued.

"Oh, Amanda. Please say that you are going to go," Hope pleaded.

"I don't know. I have to think about it."

"Well, think about it. We could go back home and see our families again," Hope said smiling.

"I have to think about it. This is sudden," Amanda said.

"Here take this," Faith said as she reached in her purse and pulled out a business card.

"This is his info. Give him a call and he would explain himself to you." "I'm going to try to go. I think he's sincere," Faith said.

She gave the card to Amanda. Amanda looked at the name on the card and stuck it in her purse.

"Okay, I'll give him a call," she said.

She walked back over to Abigail thinking about the name on the card.

"Barnabas? Is this real?" she thought.

Abigail finished with her purchase.

"Who were those girls?" she asked.

"Hope was a girl from my neighborhood. She's married now to a doctor."

"Oh, really? How nice for her," Abigail said smiling.

"And Faith is married to a musician. They came here to shop for their husbands' dinners," Amanda said trying to hide the fact that they were talking about escaping back to Earth.

"Well it looks like they settled in just fine," Abigail said looking in their direction.

"Yes, Hope told me her husband trusts her completely."

"Well, Aiden trusts you too, Amanda. It's just that he doesn't want to see you get hurt here while everything is still new to you." "I know," Amanda said.

"Aiden is a good person and I wouldn't want to disappoint him," she said as she thought about what Hope had said.

Could this be true? A way to go back to Earth.

Her heart leaped with joy, as she thought about her grandmother and Steve. She actually has a chance to go back home.

CHAPTER

Aiden was finishing up his new report on the Malatha women. He was amazed at how well they were adjusting to their new way of life. The cities were full of them. They were going to the businesses and shops like they had been on Malatha forever.

The women were getting along fine. They really enjoyed being there. Infusement treatment was doing well for the women who refused to cooperate, but it was only a few women. It seemed as though the government's plan was working. Everyone seemed happy, Aiden wrote.

"Amanda is coming along great. She seemed to open up more to me in the past few weeks. She didn't seem so closed off from me like she did in the past. She still was a little distant. I did all I could. I just have to give her a little more time. She is talking to me more, so at least I know why she is so hurt. She just has to understand that there is nothing I could have done about her grandmother and brother," Aiden thought as he rubbed his hand through his hair.

He got up from his desk and went over to the window and looked out.

He thought about the conversation they had about a week ago when she told him that she wanted to someday travel overseas when she was on earth. He thought that he would take her on a cruise to the Palinula Islands.

"She would like that," he said.

"Computer, call the Lancuchire Travel Agency."

"Yes, Lieutenant Baxter. Now calling the Lancuchire Travel Agency," the computer said.

"This is the Lancuchire Travel Agency. This is Edeva speaking. How may I help you?"

"Hello, Edeva. My name is Lieutenant Aiden Baxter, and I would like to book a cruise for two to the Palinula Islands on the last two weeks of Luna June."

"Okay, Lieutenant Baxter. We have availability on those days on our luxurious ship, the Queen Eva. Would you like to book it?"

"Yes, I would."

"What type of cabin would you like, sir?"

"I would like one with a balcony."

"Oh, that's our most luxurious one, sir. May I ask who you are going with?"

"I am going with my wife."

"Oh, she would be so happy."

"Yes, I hope so."

"You know that the islands are great at that time of year. Have you ever been there, sir?"

"Yes, I've been there once when I was a teenager."

"My parents took me there. Now I want to take my wife."

"Oh, she will be pleased."

"Okay, the trip is all booked. I will send you a confirmation email in a few minutes."

"Thank you, Edeva. You have a great day."

"Thank you, sir."

"Computer, end call," Aiden said.

"Yes, Lieutenant Baxter," the computer said.

Aiden walked back to his desk when Bartholomew and Basil walked in.

"Aiden, are you and Amanda going to Jin's place tonight?" Bartholomew asked smiling.

"No, not tonight."

"I thought we might watch a movie alone tonight. If you know what I mean?"

"Hey, it looks like you two are getting along great," Bartholomew said.

"Yeah, it seems that Amanda is really opening up to me. She told me about her life on earth. she is coming around just fine. She didn't grow up like we did. She was underprivileged on Earth. So, I want to take her traveling, because she said she always wanted to travel. That's why I booked a cruise to the Palinula Islands for the two of us. A little romantic getaway for two weeks."

"I think that will be great," Basil said.

"Yeah, she will like that," Bartholomew added.

"Yes, I hope so. I just want her to love me for me and be happy," Aiden said.

"She will buddy. She does already," Bartholomew noted.

Col. Galveston finished his call with Chancellor De Ivory and turned off his computer, then walked into Aiden's Office. He looked around at Bartholomew and Basil who stood up in attention and saluted. Aiden stood up and saluted as well.

"At ease fellows," Col. Galveston said smiling.

"Aiden did you finish that report I had you working on?"

"Yes, sir, it's all ready for you to go over," Aiden answered.

"Good. I want to look over it before my meeting with Raincourt."

"Yes, sir," Aiden said.

"You know fellows, I'm having a dinner party at my house on Saturday night, and I would love if you all will come by and bring your wives. This is my chance to introduce my wife to my colleagues. You don't have to stay long. Just drop by and meet my wife. Aiden, I especially want you to come," Galveston said seriously.

"Yes, Colonel. I will be there with my wife," Aiden said.

"Oh, what is your wife's name again?" Col. Galveston asked.

"It's Amanda," Aiden said.

"Amanda, what a lovely name."

"Yes, sir," Aiden said.

"Okay, I have to get home. My wife is cooking dinner for me. Something I have to get used to. I have to remember not to eat late lunches now that I have a wife. No more stopping at the deli." "Yes, sir," Aiden laughed.

"Well, I'll see you tomorrow," Galveston said as he walked out of the door.

Aiden stood up and put on his utility belt.

"Come on man, I'll walk you to your car," Bartholomew said.

CHAPTER

16

Aiden and Amanda walked into the family room after dinner to listen to some music. The family room was large and modern. It was filled with very pretty modern furniture. The couch sat in the middle of the room; it was a metallic silver couch. It was an L-shape sofa with buttons at the back and plush sitting pillows.

A wooden coffee table cut from a tree was in front of it, and two large armchairs that matched the couch sat opposite the couch near the glass wall and looking out into the garden. Aiden's father had an old collection of records much like the old records on Earth.

They were round and black and were made of vinyl. He played them on an old phonograph machine similar to Earth's. Aiden loved to play his father's old records. He felt that he would share it with Amanda because she was familiar with records. He thought it will make her feel at home.

He went over to the collection of records and began looking through the list of names. Amanda walked over to the far end of the room and sat in the armchair by the window wall and began staring out into the distance.

She wasn't in the mood for music tonight. What Hope told her yesterday weighed heavily on her mind all day.

"Could it be true? Could I actually go home?" she thought.

She liked Aiden and his parents, but she had to go back to earth and see what became of her grandmother and Steve.

Aiden noticed that Amanda was distant all evening at dinner. He didn't know what came over her. Why the sudden change? He asked his mother if anything happened while they were at the market yesterday, but his mother assured him that nothing happened.

Aiden found a record that his father used to play for him when he was little and he put it on.

"Here's a number I think you would like," Aiden said smiling.

"It's my father's favorite," he turned up the music and walked over to the couch and sat down.

Amanda listened to the song and her stomach turned. The women singing sounded like a little girl to her and it sounded like old music from the old days when gangsters ruled Chicago. It sounded strange and funny. It was the total opposite of R&B. She didn't want to judge their culture. In fact, she liked it, but there is no place like home. Besides, she heard the song before.

Chancellor De Ivory played it in adjustment training and it sounded funny then. She sat back on her seat, crossed her legs, and folded her arms. She looked at Aiden and rolled her eyes. Aiden noticed her attitude, but he didn't know what was the matter with her.

He tried not to get upset.

"What's the matter, Amanda? Don't you like the song?" he asked firmly looking at Amanda intensely.

"It's alright I guess, I mean, I guess I like it," Amanda responded through clenched teeth.

"Why are you seated way over there?! I'm over here, Amanda!" Aiden yelled loudly getting angry.

Amanda looked at Aiden and a fuse blew inside her.

"I just want to sit by the window!" she yelled back.

Aiden's eyes widened in surprise. He really got angry.

"Don't you yell at me! All I tried to do was make you feel welcome! I've been bending over backward ever since you got here, but all you do is shut me out!"

"I'm sorry for what happened to your grandmother and brother on Earth, but that's not my fault! This is your home now! So, you better get used to that!"

Amanda looked at Aiden who had stood up and walked over to her.

She put her hands over her face and began to cry. Aiden's heart sank.

He didn't want to hurt Amanda's feelings, but it was time that she faced the truth. All the other women seemed to accept their fate. It was time Amanda accepted hers. He stooped down and put his hand on Amanda's shoulder.

"I'm sorry. I didn't mean to hurt your feelings, but you have to accept things for what they are." We are stuck with each other. So, you better make the most of it, because there is no way out." Amanda looked at Aiden.

"Oh yes, there is," she thought as she wiped at her tears.

Abigail and Aaron came rushing into the room.

"Is everything all right, son?" Aaron asked.

"Nothing I can't handle, dad," Aiden said.

"We just had a little misunderstanding, but I got it straightened out now. We understand each other perfectly now."

"Okay, Aiden we will be in our rooms if you need us. Behave yourself and have a good night," Abigail said.

"We will," Aiden said.

Abigail and Aaron walked out of the room. Aiden looked at Amanda who was still wiping at her tears.

"She is not going to treat me this way. Why can't she be happy? I'm beginning to think I made a big mistake. Bartholomew, Basil, and Milo are so happy with their wives. Why do I have such bad luck?" Aiden thought.

Amanda looked at Aiden.

"I'm sorry for raising my voice. It's just that I miss my family and it's taken me a while to get over that. Can you forgive me?" she asked forcing a smile.

"Of course, I can," Aiden said bringing her up and hugging her.

"Now do you want to listen to some music?"

"Yes, I do," Amanda said, walking over to the phonograph machine.

"You know on Saturday, my boss is having a party and he invited us. I want you to go and wear something pretty."

Amanda's heart sank. "A party on Saturday?" she thought. "I don't want to go to a party. I want to go back home to Earth," she looked at Aiden and shook her head. "How am I going to get out of this one?" she thought. She looked through the records and saw one with the yellow label. "Love Tonight," it said in Malatha.

"Play this one?" she asked.

Aiden put it on, and the music began to play. It was soft and slow, something she could lose herself in. She closed her eyes and began to sway to the music. Aiden watched her as she listened to the song. He knew something was bothering her more than usual.

He didn't know what it was.

"Something happened at the market yesterday, and my mother isn't telling me everything. Amanda's attitude changed and I don't know what it is, but I'm going to find out," he thought.

Amanda tried to forget about all that had happened as she swayed back and forth.

"Barnabas. He might be a lifesaver, my ticket home. I have to get in touch with him, but I have to do it without Abigail finding out. I'll do it tomorrow while Aiden and Aaron are at work," she thought.

CHAPTER 17

Amanda's knees were shaking and her stomach was doing flip flops. She could hardly hold down her toast. She watched Aiden intensely as he took his time and ate his breakfast. Amanda looked at the big clock on the wall over the fireplace. It read 8:15.

Aiden had to be at work at nine o'clock but he wasn't budging. Aiden finished his toast and then got another piece from the plate in front of him. He then poured himself another cup of coffee. Amanda's hands began to shake.

She wanted Aiden to hurry up and leave. Usually, he would hurry out of the house at 7:40. He would just grab a piece of toast and rush to his car because he didn't want to be late. But today, he decided to stay for breakfast.

Aaron had already gone and Abigail had retired to her workshop. So, when Aiden finally leaves, Amanda would have the house to herself. Aiden ate the last of his toast and drank his coffee. He looked down at his watch and stood up.

"I'll be home early today. Maybe we could catch a movie," he said as he put his tablet in his briefcase.

"Okay, I want to go to Jin's place tonight," Amanda said as she stood up and went over to kiss him on the cheek. Aiden walked over to his mother's workshop door. He knocked on it and opened it.

"Mom, I'm going. I'll be back by three o'clock."

"Okay, Aiden you don't have to worry, everything will be all right," Abigail said.

"Okay, mom," Aiden said as he closed the door.

He checked his watch again and hurried for the door. Amanda watched him as he walked outside. Her heart began to race and she felt butterflies formed in her stomach. Aiden walked out of the door and headed toward the garage. Amanda hurried and put the dishes in the dishwasher then turned it on. She put the last of the food away and wiped off the table. She peeked into the workshop where Abigail was. Abigail was painting a picture at her easel.

Amanda quietly closed the door and ran into the living room. She began looking around for a telephone or some kind of calling device. She looked on the long chest, but there was no phone. Then she looked on the buffet, but she still didn't find one. She looked above the coffee table and then on the bookcase, but there was no phone or anything similar.

"Where could it be?" she thought.

She saw the door to Aaron's study. "Maybe a phone is in there," she thought. She went over to go inside. She began to push the button on the wall to slide the door open when Abigail walked into the living room.

"What are you doing, Amanda?" she asked a little startled because Amanda was about to go into her husband's study.

"Oh, I was looking for a TV or something, so I could watch a movie," Amanda said quickly trying to hide the fact that she was looking for a phone.

"Oh, it's over here in the family room. We don't keep the viewing screen in the living room, because I always thought that the family room was more comfortable," she said relieved that Amanda wasn't up to something no good.

"You're just in time. My favorite soap, Anatomy MD, is coming on. You'll love it, Amanda. It's all about doctors, nurses, patients, and medicine. You said that you wanted to go into medicine?"

"Yes, Abigail," Amanda said as she followed Abigail into the family room.

Abigail went over to a panel on the wall by the door and pushed a button. The screen came down from the ceiling. Then she grabbed the remote off the coffee table and turned the viewing screen to Channel Two.

Amanda looked at the panel on the wall and thought maybe a call button is on that panel. She thought as she went over and sat on the couch beside Abigail.

"So, are you and Aiden doing well, Amanda?" Abigail asked. "Things got a little intense last night."

Amanda's jaw dropped. "Yes, Abigail. Everything is all right. It's just that I miss home. I miss my family. Sometimes I don't think Aiden understands."

"Aiden understands. He just wants you to know that he is your family now. We all are. You are a long way from Earth and there will be no going back. So, you are stuck here with us."

"You have to give Aiden a chance. He's trying everything in his power to make you happy. If you give us a chance, you'll find that Malatha is better than Earth."

"Yes, Abigail I'll give it a chance. I do love Aiden and I appreciate everything you've done for me. I really do, but I'll try a little harder to show Aiden I love him and appreciate what he has done." "That's good, Amanda," Abigail said smiling.

"Look the show is on," Amanda looked at the screen and to her amazement, the soap opera was much like the soaps on Earth.

CHAPTER

Col. Galveston and Lieut. Baxter walked into the conference room where Chancellor De Ivory and Prime Minister Raincourt were waiting to hold a meeting on the progress of the Malatha's new citizens. They walked over to the conference table and sat down.

"Welcome gentlemen. Let's get straight to business," Raincourt said smiling.

"I want to know how things are going around Malatha with our new citizens."

"Yes, sir."

"I have a progress report that Lieutenant Baxter has written for us yesterday," Galveston said.

"And I have a report on adjustment training that I want to share with you, sir," De Ivory also stated.

"Good. Let's get to it," Raincourt said.

Galveston read off his report and he noted that the women were adjusting to Malatha's way of life better than expected.

"There were no incidents of retaliation since the first week we brought them here. Some women are beginning to settle into the jobs that were created for them and some women have signed up to go back to school after adjustment training is over."

"Besides the petty crimes that the Malatha men were doing, the women have not broken any laws as of writing. The Malatha men are also adjusting to the women well. They followed the rules when it came to obtaining a wife and they were helping the women adjust to life on Malatha. The business owners are training and hiring the women."

"In addition, our problem with violent crimes has stopped almost completely. There have been no violence-related incidents since the women arrived," Col. Galveston read.

"The military is as strong as ever. The men are reporting for duty and there is no violence in the barracks. The soldiers are taking advantage of the incentives that the government issued out for taking a wife. The new military housing was a success and the soldiers took complete advantage of it. Now we have a new military community in Surrok. I didn't expect that things will go so well quickly. Bringing the women here has solved almost all of our problems. It seems as if the women are happy they are here and the Malatha men are really doing their part in helping them adjust," Col. Galveston read as he ended his report.

"I just want to add that adjustment training is going well. Now the women could read and write Malatha. They understand our culture and our laws. They are adjusting well in their homes with their husbands. When they have a problem, they would relay it to Ambassador Johnson who then relays it to me, and I handle it the best I can. I also found out that the women were very religious on Earth and they wanted to continue their worship here on Malatha.

"I have been studying their religion, Christianity, and I found that it is similar to the old Eastern Religion Luna Fast that we have practiced for thousands of years. So, I think we should open up worship temples and allow the women to worship. That would keep them in order and help set disciplinary rules for their children to follow," De Ivory noted.

"But having a religion will bring superstition and fear into the minds of our offspring," Prime Minister Raincourt protested.

"But it will also set boundaries and help control the population," De Ivory argued.

"We can't take everything away from the women. Let them have their religion."

Raincourt thought for a moment. He turned the matter over in his mind. "Religion limits you," he thought. "But I also want discipline." "All right we can have religious temples," he finally spoke.

He looked over at Aiden who was looking down at his tablet.

"What do you think, son?" he asked Aiden.

Aiden looked up at Prime Minister Raincourt.

"I think that we should make the women feel at home as much as possible. We already took them from the only home they knew. We shouldn't take everything from them. Let them have some of their beliefs."

"They had a beautiful culture back on earth. Their music was the best in the world on Earth. If we allow them, they will bring that here. We have to give them something to sing about," Aiden said as he looked at Raincourt and then to Col. Galveston.

"I agree," Galveston said.

"My wife has a beautiful voice. She said that she used to sing at church on Earth. We can't take that away from them."

"I also agree," De Ivory said smiling. "The women sing in adjustment training and it's beautiful. Let them have their religion. I don't think it would get out of control."

"Okay, since everyone is in agreement, let it be done," Raincourt said. "Meeting adjourned."

CHAPTER

19

Amanda helped Abigail cook dinner. She wanted to try to cook a tart pudding, a recipe that she learned in adjustment training. Abigail helped her prepare the pudding, which was made of a lot of different berries. Abigail cooked a pork casserole, one of Aaron's favorite dishes. She also made a spring punch. Amanda looked at the clock over the fireplace: it was 2:30.

"Aiden will be home in half an hour. I have to call Barnabas before Aiden gets here," Amanda said.

She went to the buffet and got the dishes to set the table. Abigail took the casserole out of the oven and placed it on the server. Amanda set the table like Abigail showed her. She set Aaron's place at the head end of the table and Aiden's at the other end. She and Abigail will be seated opposite each other.

"Everything looks ready," Abigail said.

"I'm going to my workshop to finish up my painting before the men get home. If you need anything just call me, Amanda," she continued.

"Okay," Amanda said as she watched Abigail go into the room and close the door.

Amanda ran into the family room.

"I don't have much time," she whispered as she located the panel of buttons on the wall by the door. The buttons read, Viewing Screen, Music, Intercom, Windows, and Call.

She pushed the call button and a keypad came on the screen next to the panel of buttons. Amanda looked at the card Hope had given her and dialed the number. She heard a buzzing sound then a man came on the screen next to the panel. He was a medium-built man who looked Hispanic, with black hair. He had a mustache and goatee.

"May I help you?" he asked smiling.

Amanda was startled to see him looking at her.

"Ye-yes my name is Amanda. Are you Barnabas?" she asked frightened.

"Yes, I'm Barnabas. What can I do for you?" he asked.

"I heard you were going to take some women back to Earth and I would like to go."

"I am, but I won't be ready until about three weeks," he said.

"I can wait until then," Amanda said feeling uneasy.

"I have to work out all the details, but when I'm ready to go I'll let you know. Your name is Amanda?"

"Yes, that's right."

"I'll put you on my list. You have a seat on my ship. I'll take you back to Earth as well."

"Thank you."

"Oh, when you're ready to go, don't call me here. I'll call you," Amanda said trembling.

"Oh, I won't," Barnabas said, sensing the fear in Amanda.

"Don't you worry, everything is going to be all right. I'm going to get you home safe and sound. I'm risking my life to do this because I feel that it's my mission to do this. What our government did was wrong, and Mission Guardians are going to right the wrong. So, you don't have to be afraid."

"Thank you," Amanda said. "I feel better now. I'll try to call you on Monday at about the same time," Amanda said.

"That's fine, I'll be waiting for your call. Oh, and don't tell your husband or any other Malatha people. This is our secret." "I won't," Amanda said as she pushed End Call.

She looked around to see if Abigail had come out of her workshop, then she quietly walked back into the kitchen and sat at the counter. She wanted to be happy that she had a seat on the ship, but her gut told her that something wasn't quite right.

"Why does he want to risk his life helping us? I know he said that he was a missionary, but Malatha people aren't religious people, not like the people on earth. I remember Chancellor De Ivory telling us what happened to all of the churches and temples here on Malatha. I have to be careful. I have to talk to him some more before I decide," Amanda thought.

Abigail came out of the workshop to check on the food.

"Your pudding looks delicious Amanda. Aiden is going to be proud. You're really learning how to cook and handle yourself like a Malatha woman. That adjustment training is really paying off."

"Thank you. We learned a lot in the short time we've been trained. All of the women are really paying attention and we help each other out when we don't understand something. Chancellor De Ivory is nice too. He makes everything so simple, and I like to cook. I used to cook a lot back home," Amanda said.

"Well, it really shows, Amanda. I can't wait to taste your pudding. Aaron is going to like it as well. It makes the house smell like the holidays."

CHAPTER

Col. Galveston's house was full of military personnel. Chantel felt a little overwhelmed when Col. Galveston introduced her to his boss, General Ashdown. She wanted to make a good impression and she didn't want to embarrass the colonel.

Chantel spent two days getting ready for the dinner party. She spent hours looking up different Malatha dishes for the affair. She looked over at Col. Galveston who was talking to the general and De Ivory, and he let out a hearty laugh.

"Well, he seems happy," she thought.

She walked over to the long table of food to check if she needed to replace anything, but everything looked great. The door opened and two more guests came in and Col. Galveston met them in the foyer.

"Honey," he called Chantel to come over.

"This is Captain Dyer and his new wife, Dee."

Chantel shook Capt. Dyer's hand. He was a tall slender man with an olive complexion and dark black hair. She looked at Dee who was a medium-built light-skinned black woman with long black hair.

"Would you like something to eat?" she asked Dee.

"Yes, that would be nice," Dee said to Chantel. They walked over to the buffet table in the dining room.

"This is nice. Everything looks lovely," Dee said.

"Thank you," Chantel said.

"Did you do all of this yourself?"

"Yes, I researched everything on the internet."

"That was so smart."

"My husband is up for a promotion and I want to give him a little party, but I don't know where to begin."

"Well, give me a call and I will help you out," Chantel said.

"Thank you, Chantel. You are so nice."

Col. Galveston and Capt. Dyer walked into the living room which was a large room with contemporary furniture. It had a large sectional in the middle of the room, a glass coffee table in front of the section, and a glass China cabinet on the wall opposite the couch. The house had hard wooden floors throughout.

"Your home is lovely, colonel. Did your wife decorate it?"

"Yes, she picked out all of the furniture."

"The women are adapting well to their new life here on Malatha," Capt. Dyer said.

"Yes, they are," Galveston said smiling.

"My wife tries hard to please me. I didn't know how wonderful it would be to have a wife until now," he continued.

"Me either," Capt. Dyer said.

Aiden pulled up in his convertible and parked his car in front of Col. Galveston's house. He looked at Amanda, who was checking her makeup in the mirror.

"Hurry up! You made me late already!" he yelled.

"And when we get in there, you better behave! Don't embarrass me in front of my boss and Chancellor De Ivory! We are only going to be here for a little while!"

Amanda looked at him and rolled her eyes.

"I didn't want to come in the first place!" she yelled back.

"Why Amanda? Why didn't you want to come? All the other women are happy with their new life, except for you. You can't change what happened. So, you just have to accept things for what they are. So, please don't embarrass me. I have to be here. Col. Galveston told me to come.

So, grab your scarf and let's go."

Aiden got out of the car and straightened up his uniform. Amanda fixed up her dress and they walked up to the house. Aiden's heart began to pound as he walked up to the colonel's door.

"Please, if there is a god, let Amanda act right while we are here," he prayed in his thoughts as he rang the bell. Amanda's heart skipped a beat when the door opened.

Col. Galveston opened the door and smiled.

"Aiden, come in. Is this Amanda?" he asked as he shook Aiden's hand. "Yes, sir. This is Amanda."

"Amanda, this is Colonel Galveston," Aiden said as he introduced Amanda.

"Honey, this is Lieutenant Aiden Baxter and his wife Amanda," Chantel came over and shook Aiden's hand. "Isn't she pretty?" Col. Galveston said to his wife.

"Yes, she is," Chantel said smiling.

"Do you want something to eat?" she asked Amanda.

"Oh, uhm, I don't – " Amanda said hesitantly, then she looked at Aiden who gave her a stern look.

"Yes, I do," Amanda said finally.

"Well, come this way," Chantel said as she walked toward the dining room.

"You come too, Aiden and grab a bite," Col. Galveston said as they walked into the dining room.

"Aiden!" De Ivory called as Aiden walked past the living room.

"Go get a plate, Amanda. I'll be in there shortly," Aiden said to Amanda.

He walked over to De Ivory who was holding a glass of wine.

"How are things going, son?" he asked.

"Everything's alright, sir. It's just that Amanda is having a hard time adjusting to her new life."

"Oh, how so?"

"Can I talk to you about it tomorrow? Maybe you can help."

"Please come by my office first thing in the morning, son," De Ivory said.

In the dining room, Chantel showed Amanda the buffet and Amanda's stomach did flip flops as she looked at all the different food.

"Are you hungry, Amanda?" Galveston asked smiling.

"A little," Amanda said.

Aiden walked over and grabbed a plate.

"Everything looks great, sir," he said as he began putting food on his plate.

"Please, help yourself. There is plenty," the colonel said.

Amanda walked over to the corner of the room with her plate and began choosing her food. Col. Galveston looked at her and observed from afar.

"Is everything alright, Aiden?" he asked.

Aiden looked over at Amanda and exhaled.

"Everything's fine," he said. "Nothing I can't handle." He walked over to Amanda.

"Amanda, come back over here and mingle. We're only going to be here for a little while."

"I'm not even hungry," she protested.

"Well, why did you get all of that food?"

"Because Chantel gave it to me."

"Well, eat a little bit. Don't embarrass me, please." They walked back over to Col. Galveston.

"Amanda, you look young. How old are you?" the colonel asked.

"I'm eighteen," Amanda said forcing a smile.

Chantel looked at Galveston, surprised.

"Eighteen! Wow, that's young," Chantel said to Galveston.

"Well, Aiden is only twenty-five," the colonel replied.

CHAPTER

Aiden walked into his office and threw his briefcase on his desk. He took off his jacket and put it in the closet and sat down. He looked over at the clock sitting on his desk. It was exactly nine o'clock and everyone in the office was just getting settled for their long day.

Col. Galveston had not arrived yet, but he thought that he saw Chancellor De Ivory in the break room. He wanted to talk to De Ivory to get some advice about Amanda. He didn't want to get her into any trouble. His heart went out for her.

He melted every time he thought of her soft brown eyes, chocolate skin, and gentle voice. He was in love and he didn't want to do anything to hurt her. She didn't need infusement treatment. At least he didn't think she did.

It was just that something was bothering her, and she wasn't opening up to tell him what it was, the way he would have wanted her to. She was fine until she went to the market, he thought as he began typing on his keyboard.

"My mother said that she didn't do anything out of the ordinary while I was at work these past couple of days, and she hadn't been out of the house since she went to the market. But her whole attitude changed. It's like she shut down. I don't know what to do. I tried everything, but she won't talk to me. Maybe De ivory could help. But I don't want her to have infusement treatment," Aiden thought.

He looked at the clock again, it was 9:45. He thought that he had heard Col. Galveston talking in the hall. He got up, turned off his computer, walked out of his office, and went down the hall. Chancellor De Ivory was talking to Col. Galveston in his office when Aiden knocked.

"Come in," De Ivory said.

He was sitting in a chair next to the window and Col. Galveston was sitting on the couch. Aiden walked in.

"I'm sorry to bother you, sir. But if you are busy, I will come back."

"No, son. I'm not busy. I remember you asked to see me today, last Saturday at the party."

"Yes, I did," Aiden said. He looked at Col. Galveston who stood up and grabbed his jacket.

"If you want me to go so you could talk in private, I will," he said.

"No, it's nothing like that. Please, stay. Maybe you can help me as well," Aiden said.

"Are you sure?"

"Yes, sir."

"So, what's wrong with Amanda?" De Ivory asked.

"Yeah, I saw something was bothering her at the party. She seemed a little distant," Col. Galveston said.

"That's what I want to talk to you about, Chancellor," Aiden said.

He stood there for a while trying to speak as the emotions build up inside of him. His head began to spin, his chest felt tight, and his fingers began to get numb.

"Well, go on son," De Ivory said, getting concerned.

"I'm sorry. It's just that I don't know where to begin."

"Well, start from the beginning," Galveston said.

"Okay."

Aiden started from the beginning and told De Ivory and Galveston everything leading up to the party. Chancellor De Ivory looked at Col. Galveston and then at Aiden.

"So, you said she was coming around until she went out to the market?" De Ivory asked.

"Yes," Aiden answered.

"And who went to the market with her?" Galveston asked.

"My mother," Aiden answered.

"Did she meet with anyone at the shopping center?" De Ivory asked thinking maybe she met someone at the market.

"Like who? My mother said she didn't talk to anyone."

"Well, do you believe her?"

"My mother never lied to me before. I don't think she would lie to me about something like this."

"Of course not," De Ivory said smiling.

"Maybe Amanda is a little homesick. She is not being violent or anything, is she?"

"No," Aiden said.

"Did she try to run away?" De Ivory asked.

"No, she seems content. She's not fighting me or being abusive to my parents either. It's just that she seems closed off. She won't talk to me and tell me what's wrong so I can help her. She just shut me out completely. I feel like she doesn't love me like I love her and it's been five months," Aiden said looking worried.

"She acts like she doesn't know me."

Chancellor De Ivory looked at Aiden and his heart went out for him. He knew that Aiden wanted love fast, but he has to understand that sometimes, especially under these circumstances, love takes time.

"Try talking to her. Tell her that you are concerned. Be gentle and kind and if she needs counseling, I will be happy to help."

"I don't think she needs infusement treatment. She just needs a little time. She needs to get involved in an activity. What does she like to do?" De Ivory asked.

Aiden thought for a minute.

"I don't know," he finally said.

"Well send her to the Civics Center. Let her get involved with the arts. They have activities for her to do at the center. Things like art, writing, and music. That would take her mind off things. She is too idle at home, while you are away at work. She's bored. Let her get out and make some friends. It will make her feel at home. If you keep her locked away, she would feel like a prisoner," Chancellor De Ivory said.

"I know. I just worry she would get lost or worse get hurt," Aiden said. "I hope I'm not being too overprotective, he thought.

"Amanda is your partner now. You have to treat her like an equal. Treat her fair, show her how much you love her, and she will show you love in return."

"I do try to love her. It's just that she built this wall between us, and it's hard trying to knock it down. But I'll try a little harder. I won't give up without a fight," Aiden said.

"Well, just be patient with her, and if things continue, bring her in and I will talk to her personally," De Ivory said.

"Yes, sir. And, thank you, Col. Galveston for inviting me to the party. I didn't get to thank you Saturday night. The food was great, and everything was wonderful."

"Thank you, Aiden. I'm glad you were able to attend. Chantel worked very hard on all of the food and decorations. She's trying very hard to be a good wife. Amanda is young. Give her a little time and she will come around as well," Col. Galveston said.

"Yes, all of the women seem happy. I think they really want things to work out well for all of us."

"I think bringing the women here was a success," De Ivory said.

"Yes, everyone seems happy with their new wives. It's just that Amanda is a little down in the dumps, but I will do what you asked me, Chancellor De Ivory, and be patient with her. I would give it a little more time," Aiden said.

"You do that Aiden and I know things will work out. You just have to be patient and talk to her. Be her friend and show her that you really care, and she would come around," Col. Galveston said.

CHAPTER

Hope had looked through the window of the dress shop. She admired a black silk dress that she desperately wanted. The black dress was short and slender with long shears sleeve.

"I will look gorgeous in that dress," she thought.

She had told Faith to meet her at two o'clock so that they could meet Barnabas and Cyr at the sandwich shop. She checked her watch and it was already two o'clock. So, she looked around for Faith. Faith could never be anywhere on time. Ever since they began to hang out together, Faith would always be ten minutes late.

That got on Hope's nerves because she made it her business to get to places on time. She was supposed to meet Barnabas at 2:15 and she didn't want to keep him waiting. She exhaled and folded her arms, and began pacing back and forth. Her skin began to crawl. It felt like a million ants were marching down her arms.

She checked her watch. It was 2:10. Her blood began to boil.

"Hey, Hope!" Faith called from the other side of the shopping center.

Hope looked up and saw Faith running toward her with bags. Hope ran and met her halfway.

"I'm sorry I'm late, but I had to go to the market so my husband wouldn't get suspicious," Faith said.

"That's a good idea," Hope said smiling. "I was thinking about buying a new dress."

Hope checked her watch. It was time to meet Barnabas.

"Let's go to the sandwich shop," she said.

They walked through the shopping center and found the sandwich shop. They looked around and spotted Barnabas, Cyr, and Drogo sitting at the back along with other women. They walked over to them. Barnabas looked up, saw the girls and grinned.

"Hey ladies! I'm glad you could make it," he said as they stood up.

Barnabas pulled out seats for them and they sat down.

"Did you girls come alone?" he asked deceivingly.

"Yes, we came alone," Hope said smiling.

"Good. We don't want to get caught. You know the consequences."

"Yes, we do."

"I have some good news, ladies. My ship would be ready in approximately two weeks. Could you hold out until then?" "Yes," Faith said smiling.

"Good! On Friday, give me a call and I would give you all of the details."

"Do you know anyone else who wants to go? Give them my number and I will be happy to talk to them," Barnabas said smiling.

"Oh, yeah. I met this girl who was interested. She is in my adjustment training class. I told her all about you and she wants to go back to Earth with us," Faith said.

She looked around at the entrance and Donna was coming through the doors.

"There she is over there, by the entrance!" she said. Faith stood up and waved.

"Donna, over here!" she called.

Donna looked around and spotted Faith at the back. She walked over to Faith and hugged her.

"This is Donna. Donna, this is Hope, and these are the guys I was telling you about."

"This is Barnabas, Cyr, and Drogo."

"Hey, everyone," Donna greeted.

Barnabas stood up and grabbed a chair.

"So, you want to go back to Earth, why?" he asked.

"Yes, I do, because I don't feel I belong here. Earth is my home and I want to see my brothers and father again," Donna said.

"Well, it's my mission to take you back home and I'm going to do just that. What is your full name again?"

"My name is Donna Long. I'm eighteen years old. I used to live in Chicago on Earth. Now I'm married to Milo Le Grand."

"Well, Miss Long, you have a seat on my ship. Congratulations."

Donna smiled.

"Do you know anyone else who will want to go give me a call?" Barnabas asked. "Oh, and tell Amanda to call me. I see she couldn't make it."

"I'll give her a call," Hope said.

"I need a little more supplies for our journey to Earth. It's going to take me about a week to get them."

"How long do you think it would take us to go back to Earth?" Donna asked.

"About a week, it will take a few more days," Barnabas said smiling.

"We would have to be careful in leaving the port. We don't want the agents searching the ship, but once we get in the orbit and pass the atmosphere, we will be all right. Pack light. Don't bring a lot of stuff. You don't want to look suspicious. Believe me, people would notice and watch what you say. So give your husbands a good excuse for your absence, so they won't get suspicious and begin the search to look for you too soon. That would give us time to be long gone. And, be careful who you tell our secret to. If you feel that person cannot be trusted and she might blow your cover, don't tell her."

"For now, I want you to worry about yourselves and not everyone else. You are your first priority and I'm going to do my best to get you back home to Earth to your family and friends."

"Now, I have an appointment, ladies. I'll talk to you on Friday."

CHAPTER

Amanda liked to go to Jin's place. She thought that it was cool and hip. It was the one thing that reminded her of home when she was on Earth. She was too young to go to bars and drink, but here on Malatha, she wasn't a child anymore. Jin's place made her feel grown-up and independent, and she really liked the beer.

It made her feel intoxicated and free. She grabbed Aiden by the arm and ran to a table by the stage and sat down. The band was playing a fast beat and the music went through Amanda's ears and straight to her soul.

She began to clap and sway to the music and laugh hard. Aiden was happy to see Amanda in such good spirits. They didn't fight in a week. Now it's weekend and Amanda is acting like nothing has happened. She was extra nice to Aiden all week.

She made his favorite dessert, prepared his uniform for work, made his coffee, and he didn't even have to ask. She listened to his music and watched his favorite programs without a fight. She even held his hand at dinner. Maybe what he told her about accepting things for what they were got to her. Maybe it sank in or maybe Abigail's talks got to her. Whatever it was, Amanda was different, and more gentle.

The waiter came over and Aiden ordered their usual roast beef and beer.

"Do you want to dance?" Amanda asked as the band played a slow song.

Aiden got up and led her to the dance floor.

"I love this place. I'm glad we came," Amanda said as she hugged Aiden around the waist.

Aiden squeezed her tight and they swayed to the music.

"I can dance here all night," she continued.

"You are really enjoying yourself. That's great. I'm glad you seem happy," Aiden said smiling.

"I told you I like to dance," Amanda said smiling.

"I remember. Tomorrow is our fifth month anniversary and I have a surprise for you," Aiden said.

"A surprise! I love surprises. What is it?" Amanda said holding on to Aiden tight.

"Well, if I tell you, it won't be a surprise anymore," Aiden laughed.

"Well, I can't wait until tomorrow."

I can't believe it's been five months. It seems like yesterday when I first saw you in the dining hall on the ship," Aiden said smiling.

"Some of the girls are pregnant already. I wrote about it in my report at work. We should start a family soon." "Soon," Amanda said smiling.

"I want to wait until after adjustment training. We have a few more months. Then I will be all yours," she said smiling.

Aiden laughed and swung her around. Bartholomew, Basil, and Milo came into the bar with their wives. Bartholomew saw Aiden and Amanda dancing. So, they walked over and grabbed a seat near their table. The music stopped and Aiden and Amanda walked back to their seats.

"Hey, Amanda," Holly and Grace said as Amanda sat down next to them.

"How is everything going?" Amanda asked.

"Everything's great," Holly said.

"Bartholomew is taking me on a camping trip. We are going to sleep in tents and everything. He is going to teach me how to fish. I can't wait to go. I'm so excited."

"Maybe Basil and I could come along?" Grace said. "I would love to go fishing. How about you, Donna?" Grace asked.

Donna looked at Grace.

"I don't know. I'm not really an outdoors person."

"Oh, well Amanda, you and Aiden should come along."

"I would like that. I used to go fishing back on Earth with my grandfather. I think it would be nice," Amanda said.

"Then it's settled. We all will go fishing and camping.," Holly said smiling.

Donna looked at her and rolled her eyes. Amanda noticed that Donna was in a bad mood. She didn't act like her normal enthusiastic self. Amanda watched her as she sat and rolled her eyes at Holly and Grace.

Amanda didn't like Holly and Grace either, but she didn't hate them for loving their husbands. Donna acted as though she worshiped the ground Milo walked on. So why the sudden attitude? Amanda thought.

Holly was still talking about the camping trip, going on and on about the clothes she was going to wear. Amanda just nodded and smiled. Donna looked at Amanda and ran her finger around in a circle around her ear and pointed her head in Holly's direction.

Amanda tried to ignore her because she wanted to stay in good spirits. What does Donna know? She is just like them, Amanda thought to herself.

"Amanda, would you like to go to the restroom with me?" Donna asked.

Amanda looked surprised.

"Yes," she said, curious to know what Donna wanted from her.

"Aiden, would you excuse me? I'm going to the restroom," she said as she kissed Aiden on the lips.

Amanda went into the restroom with Donna. She walked up to the mirror and began combing her hair. Donna walked over to the stalls and looked at everyone, checking to see if they were alone. When she saw that they were alone, she walked up to Amanda.

"Do you know Hope and Faith?" she asked.

Amanda was surprised that she knew those names.

"Yes, I know them," she said.

"Well, you know Barnabas, Cyr, and Drogo?" Donna said smiling.

Amanda's heart jumped, but she didn't say anything.

"Oh, don't worry. I won't blow your cover. I have a seat on the ship as well. Barnabas said he missed you at the meeting at the shopping center. He told me to tell you to call him on Friday at about 2:30. He will give you the details about where to go to meet him. It's about fifty girls going so far. That includes you, Hope, and Faith," Donna said.

Amanda looked around nervously and then she nodded her head, but she didn't say anything. Donna looked at her strangely.

"Well we better go back out there, before they miss us," she said as she checked her makeup in the mirror.

CHAPTER

Chancellor De Ivory was sitting in the cafeteria of the medical building at the Surrok Army Base. He was drinking his second cup of coffee.

He had just finished an adjustment training class, the third one of the morning and he had four more scheduled in the afternoon.

He was pleased at how well the classes were going. The women were adjusting well to the Malatha way of life. Five months have passed and there had been no major problems, not since the first month. Almost all of the women were spoken for and the Malatha men seemed to be pleased at how well things were going.

Everyone seemed to have a wife, both in the military and the civilians. Everyone had one except De Ivory. He was too busy matching everyone else. He didn't choose a wife for himself, but he had his eye on a woman in his adjustment training class that he thought was really special.

She was a mature woman who used to be a nurse on Earth. De Ivory thought that she was pretty and smart. He saved her for himself. She still lived at the compound. He thought that he might choose her first thing Monday morning. He already had a big house. But when he bought it, he never thought of filling it with children.

Now, it didn't sound like a bad idea. He thought about the possibility when he was on Earth, but he was too busy organizing everything to choose a wife for himself. Now that adjustment training is almost complete, he has the time for a wife and possibly a child or two.

He took a bite of his sandwich and said her name to himself.

"Estelle Cook. That is a pretty name. Humans have such pretty names and they are easy to pronounce," he said.

His heart fluttered when he thought about her. He couldn't get her face out of his mind. He remembered the conversation they had the other day. She was talking to him about the different plants on the lawns of the compound and how they were similar to those on Earth.

She loved the climate there on Malatha for it was warmer than Chicago. De Ivory thought that he might take her to the beach, where she could take in even more sun. He smiled at the thought of walking on the beach with her, hand in hand. She knew a lot about the human anatomy. That knowledge could come in handy. He thought about getting her a job at the medical building working with the soldiers.

He took out his tablet and began going over his notes for the next class when a shadow came over him. It blocked his light. He looked up and it was Tobias Crump, an enlistee, a cook in the dining hall.

"Chancellor De Ivory, may I talk to you for a minute? It is very important," he asked.

De Ivory looked at him. He was a short stout man with short black hair and olive skin.

He motioned for Tobias to sit down.

"I'm sorry to bother you, sir. I know that you are busy, but what I have to say is pretty important," Tobias said, looking wide-eyed at De Ivory.

"Go on," De Ivory said, getting impatient.

"Did you know that there is a plan to kidnap some of the women and take them to Cyprus Five where they would be sold into sex slavery?" De Ivory's jaw dropped.

"Who is going to try something like that?!" he shouted.

Tobias put his finger up to his lips.

"Shhh!" he whispered.

"It's these three guys. One of them is an ex-military. His name is Barnabas Drapers and he is working on this ship big enough to take as many women as he could. Barnabas asked me to get him all the information that I could on the women so he would know as much about them as possible. He is planning on taking them in two weeks," Tobias said.

He gave De Ivory all of the details about the kidnapping and De Ivory wrote it all down.

"About fifty women are going so far," Tobias said.

De Ivory was at a loss for words. He couldn't believe that someone would try something so heinous.

He had to call an emergency meeting and stop Barnabas in his tracks.

"I warned the men of Malatha that if any harm comes to any of the women, there will be consequences, but there is always someone willing to try anything to make a fast buck," De Ivory thought.

"Thank you, Tobias," he said as he gathered his things.

"I have to go," he said. "If you come across any more information, give me a call."

"I will, sir," Tobias said.

De Ivory grabbed his briefcase and ran to the cafeteria door. His heart was beating fast.

"I have to stop this! This is bad!" he thought.

He turned and looked at Tobias.

"If you have anything else, please let me know!" he shouted as he turned and ran out of the door.

CHAPTER 25

Chancellor De Ivory called an emergency meeting with Prime Minister Raincourt and his cabinet members. He told them about the plan that Barnabas Drapers plotted to kidnap some of the women and take them to Cyprus Five to sell them into sex slavery. The cabinet members were shocked. Prime Minister Raincourt was furious.

"When is this supposed to take place?!" he shouted.

"In about two weeks," De Ivory answered.

"My informant was very sure about the details."

"Who is this informant?" Col. Galveston asked.

"He is an enlistee. He was on the mission to go to Earth to retrieve the women. He is an honest person. I've known him for a long time. He wouldn't lie to me."

"Do you know the names of the women who are planning to go on this trip?" Col. Galveston asked.

"He did not tell me that. He said that Barnabas had about fifty women so far," De Ivory said.

Aiden was surprised and angry about the news he was hearing. He wondered if Amanda knew anything about Barnabas. He took notes and listened to De Ivory very carefully.

"We need to arrest Barnabas before he harms those women," De Ivory said.

"No, we will send some men to spy on Barnabas and gather all the information they could on the women. And on the date of their departure, we will arrest them. That way Barnabas will be caught red-handed with the women as evidence, and then we could prosecute him with the maximum penalty, and the women –we would give them infusement treatment," Prime Minister Raincourt said.

"What is the maximum penalty for a crime like this?" Aiden asked.

"Death!" Prime Minister Raincourt shouted.

"It's in the bylaws that if any man tries to undermine the laws governing the women, their penalty will be death."

Aiden looked at Prime Minister Raincourt.

"What about the women?" he asked. "They think they are going back to Earth."

"Well the laws for them are the same. Because they refused to adjust to the Malatha way of life and they tried to escape, they will get infusement treatment," Prime Minister Raincourt said.

"So, all you men, who have new wives should warn them about this before they get caught trying to escape," he continued.

"I will discuss this with my class in the upcoming days," De Ivory said.

"I will assign the soldiers from tactical, who will be the undercovers," Col. Galveston said.

"I know a few who could get the job done without detection," he continued.

"I would tell my informant to gather as much information on Barnabas as he could," De Ivory said. "I am not comfortable giving you his name just yet, but I know he is a good person. I matched him up with a wife a couple of months ago, and he got military housing. So, I know he isn't trying to scam the women," De Ivory said.

"Well, have you asked him to get the names of those women? We need to know so we could at least know who they are," Col. Galveston asked.

"I will," De Ivory said.

Prime Minister Raincourt brought Barnabas' picture on the large computer screen on the wall.

"Barnabas Drapers, was he an ex-military?" he asked as he looked at his picture on the screen.

"Yes, he was a damn good soldier. He was a pilot on the space task force and a good sniper. He served fifteen years before he got wounded in the leg, ending his career. He retired with an honorable discharge," Col. Galveston said.

"He earned a medal of honor and a bronze star for his injuries. Now, he flies a cargo ship hauling cargo from sector to sector. His parents are dead, and he has a younger brother named Drogo, who works with him on his ship," Galveston continued.

"So, he knows a lot about Cyprus Five and their sex slave operation?" Prime Minister Raincourt asked.

"Yes, and they pay a lot for those women they gathered from all around the galaxy. We really have to put a stop to this and give Barnabas the maximum penalty, before someone else tries this," Galveston said.

"Yes, he needs to be stopped and we will make his trial public. So, all of Malatha will know what the consequences are for messing with the government," Prime Minister Raincourt said.

Aiden couldn't help but think about Amanda. He hoped that she wasn't among the women who were going with Barnabas. He was going to talk to her when he got home. She had been acting angry earlier in the month, but now she is fine. They haven't had a fight in about a week, he thought. He was going to tell Bartholomew and the guys would go to talk to their wives about Barnabas so they won't get into any trouble.

Prime Minister Raincourt looked at De Ivory.

"Well, have we covered everything?" he asked.

"Yes, I think we did," De Ivory said.

"Well, if there aren't any more questions, the meeting is adjourned."

CHAPTER 26

Barnabas, Cyr, and Drogo were storing supplies in the cargo bay of the ship. The engine was almost ready. Barnabas needed one more part, which would be in on Friday. They had all their supplies enough for a month's journey to Cyprus Five and back.

Barnabas couldn't believe how easy it was to round up fifty women. Cyprus Five paid well for good and healthy humanoid women, he thought. And that was what he was going to deliver to them.

He didn't think about what sex slavery would do to the women or how they felt about being abducted by the Malatha military. He only thought about how much money he was going to make for each woman he sold into slavery.

Cyr was all aboard with his plan. He was as ruthless as Barnabas. He couldn't care less about how this might affect the women or their husbands. He needed money and he needed it quick and easy.

Drogo, on the other hand, hated the idea. He felt bad that Barnabas would stoop so low. He thought that it was a good idea to bring the women to Malatha to be brides to the lonely men who live there.

He wanted a wife himself, but now he is going to be on the run with Barnabas and Cyr.

"Do you think the women are going to know about our plan, Barnabas?" Drogo asked curiously.

"No, we have been talking to them for three weeks now and they haven't caught on yet. Don't worry, Drogo. This is a foolproof plan. No one knows but us," Barnabas said.

"The women know," Drogo said.

"Yes, they know, but they won't tell anyone. They want to go home to Earth, and as far as they know, we are taking them back."

"It just seems too easy, Barnabas," Drogo said as he stacked a crate on top of a stack of crates on the back wall.

"You know when things seemed easy, something always goes wrong," he continued.

"Don't worry Drogo, nothing will go wrong. Just do what I tell you and we will be all right. I've never let you down in the past, have I?" Barnabas asked.

"No, Barnabas, you haven't," Drogo said as he looked down at his shoes.

"Well, I won't let you down this time. On the day of the departure, we are going to get the girls on the ship and take off before anyone notices. Once we pass the solar system, we'll be in deep space. You know how long that would take?" Barnabas asked.

"Fifteen minutes," Drogo answered.

"Yes, remember that the ship would be like new with those engine parts."

Cyr was listening as he was taking inventory of the supplies. He checked to see if they had enough spacesuits for all of the women, just in case of an emergency. He checked the medical supplies. He checked to see if they had enough plasma fuel for the engine.

They had a month's supply. Everything seemed to be in order. They had food and water. He checked their weapons and their weapons were already good to go. He checked the torpedo launcher of the ship and it was in order.

"Everything is ready to go," he said to Barnabas, who was going over the list of names one more time.

"Are you sure you have everything, Cyr?" Barnabas asked.

"Yes, I checked everything, But I can't think of anything else. Anyway, the sleeping quarters are in order. We have blankets and pillows. The restrooms are in order as well. Yep, everything on the list is in order."

"Good, then we are good to go," Barnabas said smiling. "This is going to be a piece of cake," he continued.

"I can't wait to count all of my cash," Cyr said rubbing his hands together. "We are going to be rich," he continued.

"Do you think we should give Tobias a cut?" Drogo asked.

"No, he didn't ask for anything. He owes me a favor and you know how I am about paying me back."

"Do you think he would tell?" Drogo asked.

"No, Tobias is a good friend. I've known him for over twenty years. He won't turn me in. Besides, if we do get caught, I'll tell them he gave me military information. He could be court-martialed for that. And he wouldn't want that. So, my secret is safe with him. I have to go to my office. It's almost time for the women to call me."

Barnabas walked out of the cargo bay and down a long hallway to an elevator. He got on the elevator and pressed the button to the bridge. The elevator went to the bridge. He got off and went to his office. He sat at his desk and waited for his first phone call to come in. The phone rang and he brought Hope on the screen.

He liked Hope; she was pretty and cheerful, and she always had a smile for him. If he was interested in a wife, he would choose someone like Hope, but he wasn't so sure she will make an excellent sex slave.

CHAPTER

The flowers in the garden were in every color in the rainbow. There were red ones, yellow ones, and blue ones. The grass was a deep sea of green and there wasn't a cloud in the sky. The day was perfect. The air was nice and warm on Amanda's face.

She loved walking through the garden at the back of Aiden's house. Abigail had planted a really beautiful garden that everyone in the neighborhood envied. The backyard was big and spacious – two whole acres of trees, plants, and flowers.

Amanda walked through the garden taking in the scenery while Abigail made lunch. It was Friday and she had to call Barnabas, but how was she going to get away from Abigail long enough to do that. She checked her watch. It was exactly twelve o'clock.

"I have to know where to meet them. I need all of the details. Donna didn't tell me much. How am I going to get away from Aiden on the night of the departure? Aiden really loves me. I could see it in his eyes. I don't want to hurt him, but I have to see my grandmother again," she thought.

Abigail came out with a tray full of sandwiches and a bowl of salad. Amanda walked over to the table and sat down.

"Everything looks nice, Abigail," Amanda said.

"Thank you, Amanda. I enjoy eating outside on the patio on days like this."

"Yes, it really is a nice day," Amanda said.

"So, what do you and Aiden have planned for tonight?" Abigail asked.

"I don't know. Aiden said that it is a surprise, but I can't wait! I love surprises," Amanda said smiling.

"That's good. I noticed that you and Aiden have been getting along pretty good lately. I'm glad. So, have you taken my advice?" Abigail asked.

"Yes ma'am, I have. I love Aiden and I don't want to do anything to hurt him. Besides, it's not his fault I'm here. This is a lovely home and you and Aaron are good people. I'm lucky to be here with you. Thank you for having me."

Abigail listened to Amanda. She heard how sincere she was, and her heart went out for her.

"You are welcome, baby. Here, have some more salad."

Amanda got another sandwich and some salad, and continued eating.

"I'm going to dress up for Aiden tonight. I want to look good for the surprise," she said.

Abigail smiled as she looked down at her tray.

"Oh, you know what. I forgot the cookies. They are sitting on the kitchen counter."

"Oh, I'll get them," Amanda said. "I have to use the bathroom anyway. I'll be right back."

Amanda got up, hurried into the house, and closed the door. She hurried into the family room and pressed the call button on the panel on the wall. Barnabas came on the screen.

"Amanda, I was waiting for your phone call," he said smiling.

"I'm sorry I had to get away. I can't talk long. Abigail is waiting for me in the backyard," Amanda said looking toward the kitchen.

"Okay, I'll just give you the details. We are going to meet next Friday night at the ship port. We'll be at the ship dock from seven to eight o'clock. Pack light and don't bring a lot of stuff. If you need an excuse to get out of the house, tell your husband that you are going to take a cooking class at the Civics Center. He should let you go and that would buy us time to depart. That's what the other girls are telling their husbands. So, I hope to see you next Friday night. Goodbye," Barnabas pressed End Call and the screen went dark.

Amanda hurried to the kitchen, grabbed the cookies off the counter, and took them outside.

"Here they are," she said to Abigail who was finishing up her salad.

"These cookies look great! You have to show me how to make them," Amanda said smiling.

"These are Aiden's favorite. I will show you how to make them," Abigail said.

"Remember when you told me about that class at the Civics Center? I think I want to join so I can learn how to cook Malatha dishes for Aiden. So, when we get our own place, he won't be so homesick," Amanda said.

"I think that would be a good idea. He would like that, Amanda. But you know what? You are a good cook already. You don't need to take any classes."

Amanda's eyes widened. She had to think fast.

"I want to get better. I want to know all there is to know about Malatha cooking."

Abigail smiled.

"That's good, dear. Why don't you get Holly and Grace to take the classes with you? I know they would enjoy it," Abigail said.

"That sounds like a good idea. I'll ask them tomorrow when I see them again."

"I was thinking maybe I'll take a writing class too. It will give me something to do while Aiden is at work," Amanda said smiling, relieved that Abigail bought her excuse. She took a deep breath and exhaled.

CHAPTER

28

The light from the amusement park was brightly illuminating against the night sky. Amanda could see it from a distance as they drove toward it in Aiden's hovercar. Her heart danced when Aiden told her that they were going to Cosmic World, one of the biggest amusement parks in Surrok.

Amanda had never been to an amusement park, not even on Earth. She always wanted to go to Six Flags Great America, but she never got the chance to go, not even on a school trip. Her jaws hurt from the grin that ran across her face. All she wanted to do was hug and kiss Aiden for being so thoughtful.

She could see the different attractions as they got closer to the park. She jumped excitedly and clapped her hands. She grabbed Aiden by the arm and kissed him on the cheek. Aiden's heart skipped a beat and he grinned as he watched how excited Amanda had gotten.

He held tight to the steering wheel and tried to drive safely down the road. They drove into the parking lot and Aiden found a parking space near the entrance.

"This is so cool!" Amanda shouted as they got out of the car.

"This is your surprise?! How did you know I wanted to go to an amusement park?" she asked holding on to Aiden's arm.

"I just figured you would like it since you liked going to the beach so much. My parents used to take me here almost every weekend when I was little. Now we can take our children," Aiden said smiling.

"I love you Aiden. You always know what makes me happy," Amanda said as she hugged Aiden.

"Let's get inside. I want to try every ride!"

They walked up to the gate and Aiden showed the attendant his pass as they went inside. The park was vast, with colorful whimsical attractions all around the place. Amanda could hear people laughing and screaming from different directions.

The ground was made of brown cobblestone. A yellow road was at the center of it, and that led paths around the park. The first ride Aiden took Amanda to was an old wooden roller coaster with a long drop to the bottom.

"This was my mother's favorite ride. She would let me ride this every time we came here," Aiden said grinning.

They got in the line and Amanda watched the roller coaster slowly make its way up the ramp. When it got to the top, it sped down the drop and made a turn around a circle at the bottom, and began slowly up a slightly smaller ramp.

Amanda's eyes widened as the coaster dropped, then butterflies foamed in her stomach. She shook her head in disagreement.

"No, I don't think so, Aiden. That coaster looks dangerous!" Aiden looked at her.

"Don't worry it's safe. I'll hold your hand," he said laughing.

"Then we'll both die together!" Amanda said squeezing Aiden's hand.

"I won't let you get hurt. In fact, this is a baby roller coaster. Look at that one over there," Aiden said pointing to another larger coaster.

Amanda looked over to the roller coaster behind her. It was made like a rocket with steel tracks that went up in the air, around four times in a loop, and then dropped down. Her eyes got wide and she shook her head no.

"That's a death trap!"

Aiden broke out in laughter. "It will be fun," he insisted as the line moved closer to the entrance of the roller coaster.

Amanda's stomach was turning upside down after the last ride of the night. She thought that she was going to die after the Rocket Coaster, but Aiden had managed to talk her into riding almost every ride in the park.

Her head was spinning, and her heart was pounding. All she wanted to do was go home, take a hot bath, and crawl into bed.

"Now that we've conquered Cosmic World, where do you want to go eat?" Aiden asked grinning.

"Eat! How could you think about eating after all of that? I don't think I could hold down any food at this point," Amanda protested. Aiden laughed loud.

"All of those rides made me hungry," he said teasing. "I know where we could go get a footlong sandwich, some chips, and beer," he continued.

Amanda wanted to throw up, but she grabbed onto Aiden's arm and he led her out of the amusement park, and into the parking lot. She looked back one last time at Cosmic World and thought about what she was going to tell her grandmother.

Aiden had too much fun. He didn't think about Barnabas anymore. After work, he didn't believe that Amanda would try to run away from him. She loved him too much, so he thought.

CHAPTER

Everything was quiet during the drive to the sandwich shop. Amanda was taking in the scenery. She loved driving at night. The moon was big, yellow, and bright and the sky was filled with stars as far as the eye could see. She saw shapes in the stars, but not like the shapes in the sky on Earth. Aiden noticed that Amanda's mind was occupied by the night sky, but the silence was killing him. It was hollow and thick, like a big dark empty room.

He had to have a conversation to cut the clutter in his head, or else the silence would kill him.

"Amanda, are you enjoying the ride?" he asked, trying to start a conversation.

"Yes, I was looking at the stars, trying to see the shapes."

"Do you have constellations on this planet?" she asked curiously.

"Yes, we have constellations. We have a polar star that our sailors use to navigate their ships by. Look over there. That is the big fish," Aiden said, pointing to the sky.

Amanda looked up.

"I see it! It looks just like a fish."

"And over there is the little fish. And that constellation over there is Queen Ella. She was a queen about a thousand years ago. She was supposed to have lost her baby and was said to be looking for him in the night sky," Aiden continued.

"If you are interested in the constellations, I have a book I can give you. It will tell you all about the night sky," Aiden said smiling, trying to keep the conversation going.

"That will be great. I used to enjoy reading about the night sky on Earth. I used to know all about the Big Dipper and the Little Dipper. I used to go to the planetarium a lot too. Because the lights were too bright in the city, you couldn't see much stars at night. So, I'd read about them in books I used to borrow from the library. But it is beautiful here. You can see all the stars really well."

"Yes, we have no need for big bright lights here. We used to in the past, but crime isn't as bad as it used to be a few hundred years ago, and now we could enjoy our world and all it has to offer. I'm glad you are enjoying yourself," Aiden said as he parked the car in the parking lot of the sandwich shop.

"Are you hungry?" he asked.

"Yes, I am. I could eat a horse," Amanda said laughing.

Aiden leaned over and tried to kiss her on the lips. Amanda noticed him leaning forward and turned her head away. Aiden was surprised and saddened at her sudden move.

"What's wrong Amanda?" he asked as he gripped the steering wheel until his knuckles turned white.

"There is nothing wrong," Amanda said as she unbuckled her seatbelt. "I'm just not in the mood."

"What do you mean you are not in the mood? You are never in the mood!" Aiden said through clenched teeth.

"We are married! All I want is a little kiss!" he continued, throwing up his hands.

"We kiss. I kiss you! It's just that it's dark and cold, and I'm hungry. I don't feel like it right now!"

"Well, tell me when you are going to feel like it, because you haven't felt like it for a while now!" Aiden yelled as his body shook all over.

"You're just going to have to give me a little time. Sometimes I feel like you are suffocating me!" Amanda yelled as anger builds up inside of her.

Aiden's jaw dropped. It felt like his head was going to blow up when he heard those words. He jumped in his seat and tightened his fist, and frowned at Amanda.

"Suffocating!" he yelled.

"All I ever tried to do was be nice to you. I tried to show you that I love you and you call that suffocation! You are really full of yourself! How could you be so self-centered! You are unbelievable!" he yelled as he got out of the car.

He began walking down the road. He didn't want to deal with Amanda anymore, or he would do something he would regret. So, he kept walking. Amanda sat in the car. She didn't know why she said those things.

She didn't want to hurt Aiden. She just wanted to keep her distance until it was time to meet Barnabas. She had to be cool and go with it until she got a chance to leave.

"If I keep acting this way, he is going to find out everything. I got to keep my cool," she thought.

Aiden walked down the road and then he remembered that he left his engine running. So, he walked back slowly.

"How could she say those things to me?" he asked. "I thought things were finally going well between us, but every time I tried to get a little close, she pulls away! What am I supposed to do?" he asked himself.

He opened the door to the car and stepped inside. Amanda looked at him with tears in her eyes.

"I'm sorry Aiden," she said. "You don't suffocate me. I don't know why I said that to you. I love you."

Aiden looked down. He pulled out of the parking space and started driving.

"I know," he said as he drove down the street.

CHAPTER 30

"The Mark 37-P Laser Rifle is the most advanced of its kind. It hits its target with one hundred percent accuracy. All you have to do is aim and fire. It is lightweight, so it is easy to handle, and it stores well until you need it," Ives De Grey said to Barnabas who was looking to buy some up-to-date weapon.

Barnabas picked up one of the rifles and held it in his hands as if he was going to fire it.

"It is lightweight," he said as he looked it over.

"Yes, this is the best of its kind. It is a military issue. This is the rifle the space task force uses," De Grey said smiling.

"We can use a few of them. How much do you want for them?" Barnabas asked.

"How many do you need?" De Grey asked.

Barnabas looked down at the case of rifles.

"I need about three," he said.

"This will run you about three thousand gelts," De Grey said as he picked up two more rifles.

"This is a nice ship. Looks like you are going on a venture."

"We are hauling some cargo to Cyprus Five. Nothing out of the ordinary. It's pretty routine," Barnabas said.

"Oh, why the weapons?" De Grey asked.

"We ran into some Rusen pirates in Quadrant Five the last time we were out that way. I want to be prepared next time. I can't lose this cargo. It's too valuable," Barnabas answered.

"Oh, what is it? If you don't mind me asking."

"Oh, some much needed plasma fuel for the Cyprus Five Outpost Station. You know fuel is hard to get way out there."

"I see," De Grey said. He walked around the deck of the ship and saw the stacks of food and blankets, and other supplies.

"It looks like you are going to be gone for a year," he said to Barnabas.

"No, we are going to be gone for about a month," Barnabas said.

"Why so much food?"

"They're for my men. They eat a lot and some of these are for emergencies. You never know with this old ship," he said.

Barnabas hurried up and got the three thousand gelts and paid De Grey. De Grey then gave him the three rifles he purchased. He closed up his case and headed for the exit. Barnabas went with him to make sure he got off the ship. Cyr put the weapons in the weapon case and closed them up.

"He asked a lot of questions, Cyr," Drogo said. "He might be suspicious."

"Don't worry about it. He doesn't know anything. He is just a thief, like us," Cyr said.

Barnabas came back into the room and sat at the mess hall table and laughed.

"Is he gone?" Drogo asked.

"Yes," Barnabas answered.

"That was close! I thought he knew," said Drogo, wiping his hand across his forehead.

"Don't worry, Drogo. No one knows. He was just trying to make conversation. You have to stay cool," Barnabas said.

"Yeah. No one will know unless you tell them," Cyr said as he went over the list of supplies one more time.

"Well, Friday is in three days and this will be all over," Barnabas said. "I can't wait until then," Drogo said.

"This is nerve-wracking! Have you heard from the ladies?" Cyr asked.

"Yes, I talked to them last night. They are all ready to go. We just have to lie low until Friday," Barnabas said smiling.

"I got in touch with Dork and I told him how many women we have going, and he said that he would pay healthy for humanoid women. There's a big demand for them on Cyprus Five," he continued.

"We are going to be rich!" Cyr said smiling.

"Yes, we are," Drogo said.

Barnabas got up, went to his office, and sat down on his desk. When the phone rang, he answered it. Tobias came on the screen.

"Tobias, what can I do for you?" Barnabas asked.

"I want to download for you the Earth women human anatomy chart. It was on my itinerary and I thought you might need it," Tobias said smiling.

"I do! That might come in handy on Cyprus Five," Barnabas said. "Send it to me, please. We are going to depart on Friday at eight in the evening. All of the women will be here," Barnabas continued.

"Oh, how many do you have going now?" Tobias asked.

"Oh, over seventy-five women. I was pushing for a hundred, but my ship is small. So, I stopped at seventy-five," Barnabas said smiling.

"Well, I have to go Tobias," Barnabas said as he pushed End Call.

Tobias ended the call and turned to De Ivory, who was standing on the other side of the room.

"He has seventy-five women now, Chancellor," he said.

"I know Tobias, I know," Chancellor De Ivory replied.

CHAPTER

Chancellor De Ivory was sitting at his desk, looking at the pictures of Barnabas Drapers' ship. Special Forces Lieut. Ives De Grey had taken them the day before while he was meeting with Barnabas. De Grey is an efficient soldier, just the right man to get information on Barnabas. He was assigned to do just that by Col. Galveston.

"He took the bait and bought the Mark 37-P Laser Rifle, sir, but he has other weapons in his arsenal," De Grey reported.

He gave De Ivory a picture of the deck of the ship with the cargo, and a picture of the living quarters.

"His ship is large enough to hold at least a hundred women, and he had it filled with food and supplies. He is planning on being gone for at least a month, sir," De Grey continued.

De Ivory looked at the pictures over and over.

"We have to stop this guy. How could he try such a thing?" De Ivory said angrily.

He rubbed the back of his neck and a tingling sensation went through them as he took a short deep breath to calm himself.

"He's doing it for the money, sir. My informant on Cyprus Five told me that he got in touch with a guy named Dork, who was willing to pay heavily for the women," De Grey said in disgust.

"Dork? Who is this Dork fellow?" De Ivory asked as he felt like he was going to throw up.

"He is a low life scumbag who owns a strip joint, and he runs a prostitution ring on Cyprus Five. He hides under the protection of Cyprus Five's laws of legalized prostitution, and he thinks he can't be touched. He dare not go off the planet because he is wanted by the universal galaxy of planets," De Grey said.

"Well, if he harms any of my girls, I'm going to personally bring him here and kill him," De Ivory furiously replied.

Col. Galveston came into the office, walked over to the couch, and sat down. Ives De Grey stood up and saluted.

"At ease, lieutenant," Col. Galveston said.

"Just look at these pictures, Bardolph," De Ivory said. "They're appalling! Look at these women. I know them from adjustment training," he continued, handing Galveston the pictures with shaking hands. Col. Galveston looked at the pictures to see if Chantel knew any of the women.

"How many women does he have so far?" the colonel asked.

"He has seventy-five. Seventy-five of the dumbest women I've ever seen," De Ivory answered in disgust.

"He is supposed to depart at Dock 7 on Friday at eight o'clock. We will be ready and wait for the women to arrive," De Grey said.

"I'm getting the holding cell ready for the women. When they come in, the doctors will be ready to give them infusement treatment, which is a shame because it takes several months to get over the treatment," De Ivory said.

"Will they ever get over the treatment and go back to their old personality?" De Grey asked.

"No, they would never be like they were before, but they could live normal lives," De Ivory answered.

Galveston looked at De Ivory and saw the hurt in his eyes.

"Don't worry, De Ivory. Don't let this get to you. We are going to stop Barnabas and we will see that no one else tries to do this ever again. I'm concerned for you. If you let this stress you out, you will get ill," Col. Galveston said to his friend.

"I'm okay. It's just that I worked so hard to bring those women here and I don't want to see them hurt. Our intention wasn't to hurt or abuse them. I thought I was giving them a good home here with us men who appreciate them," he continued.

"And you did."

"Those women who signed up to go with Barnabas are not even a fraction of the millions of women you brought here. They won't even be missed, but we have to show the other women that they have to obey, or they will face the consequences," Galveston said.

"So, we are going to make an example out of those women so that the others won't dare try to do that. Ever," he continued.

"I have to inform Prime Minister Raincourt about the new information. He is anxious to know what's going on. So, I have to tell him that we will be ready on Friday," Galveston said.

"So, how is Estelle? I see you put off choosing her for your wife," Galveston said smiling. De Ivory smiled back.

"Yes, for now. I'm going to choose her after all of this blows over. I have to give this matter my undivided attention, but soon as we have Barnabas behind bars, I'm going to sign the contract," De Ivory said while his heart fluttered.

"That's great, Chancellor. You deserve a little happiness. My wife is great. I never thought how much I needed someone until I got married," De Grey said.

"Yes, I agree. Chantel means the world to me too. You are going to love having someone, De Ivory," Galveston said.

"So, don't put it off too much longer. We have to get on with our lives," he continued.

De Ivory looked at the pictures on his desk one more time.

"Yes, we have to get on with our lives, but first I want to deal with Barnabas.

CHAPTER

32

Aiden looked at Amanda's soft long black hair, her oval-shaped face, her ruby red lips, and her shapely round breasts; he felt his pulse race. His heart banged on the walls of his chest and his knees felt weak.

He was in love and there was no denying it.

The lights were dim in the restaurant and the candles on the table were illuminating a soft glow around Amanda's head. She looked like an angel. Aiden smiled and reached for her hand. She put her hand in his hand and smiled.

Aiden was tall and olive-skinned, with thick black straight hair. He was strong and sure of himself. He was the first man Amanda knew. She didn't care anymore that he wasn't an Earth human or black. She loved him more than she could ever imagine.

Aiden squeezed her hand and her heart burst in her chest. The music was soft and gentle, and Amanda's brain fizzled. She didn't want this night to end. Even though she wanted to see her grandmother and Steve again, she didn't want to leave Aiden or the city of Surrok. It was enchanting there. She did things she never would have gotten to do on Earth. Now she is in love, and she didn't care who knew it.

The waiter came to take the order. Aiden looked up at him.

"Will you give us a second?" he asked.

The waiter walked over to another table. Aiden found Amanda's eyes and looked deeply into them.

"We better order before they take our table," he said.

Amanda laughed and looked down at her menu.

"I think I would have the stew," she said smiling.

"I will too," Aiden said as he motioned for the waiter.

"We will have two bowls of your stew," Aiden said to the waiter as he took their order.

"What would you like to drink with that?" the waiter asked.

"A bottle of red wine," Aiden said smiling.

The waiter went to the back with their order.

"You look amazing tonight, Amanda," Aiden said, reaching for her hand again.

"Thank you. You look nice too. Thank you for bringing me here. This is a nice restaurant," Amanda said as she looked around at the square tables, the mosaic walls, and the marble floors. She looked out of the large bay window overlooking the ocean. The moon was bright, shining a soft white light on the water.

"Do you want to dance?" Aiden asked as he got up and led her to the dance floor.

The music was slow and soft. Aiden pulled Amanda close and they swayed to the music. Aiden's breath was warm on Amanda's cheek and a lovely scarlet flush colored her chocolate complexion. She closed her eyes and lost herself in the music.

"Are you enjoying yourself?" Aiden asked as he whispered in her ear. His words sent an electric jolt through Amanda's body.

"I am," she said as she leaned into him. He held her tight with his strong long arms.

He didn't want to let her go. Her hair smelled like berries and her skin was like silk, sending Aiden's manhood into attention. He pulled her close and kissed her on the cheek. Amanda smiled, wanting more.

They swayed together in rhythm with each other's body as the music played a soft and light beat.

"This is one of my favorite songs," Aiden whispered, his lips touching Amanda's ear.

"I like it too," she said as she looked in Aiden's big brown eyes.

"I'm glad," Aiden said smiling. "I don't want to lose you, Amanda. I love you too much."

Amanda looked at him.

"You're not going to lose me. I'm going to be with you forever. Thank you for loving me, Aiden," she said.

She thought about Barnabas and her grandmother. She wanted to see her grandmother again. Barnabas could take her back to earth. She just had to try to go back. She didn't want to hurt Aiden. She loved him, and she loved Aaron and Abigail too, but she had to know what became of her grandmother and brother.

Steve was young and he couldn't take care of himself. She had to go and see him. She had to. Aiden pulled her close and kissed her on the cheeks, and she melted. He then found her mouth and they kissed.

Amanda's heart exploded as she kissed Aiden back. She sank into his body instantly. The hard planes of his muscle enfolded her. Aiden's lips intertwined with hers sent his body into ecstasy. He didn't want to stop kissing her. Amanda wanted him inside of her more than anything she ever wanted before.

CHAPTER

Aaron Baxter was sitting in the family room reading the news on his tablet. The reports about the new women of Malatha interested him the most. He was delighted that they were immigrating so well. He had begun to see them everywhere. They walked around and lived as if they were in Malatha forever.

Some were even doing jobs at Aaron's workplace. It was strange to have women everywhere, but a good kind of strange. To Aaron's surprise, the women didn't cause any trouble. They fit into society like they were always supposed to be.

Aaron thought about Amanda and how she became part of the family. It was like she always belonged.

"Aiden is happy. I see how he loves Amanda. They had problems in the beginning, but now they get along just fine," he said to himself.

He read in the news how some women were going to study medicine and he thought that would interest Amanda. She had told him and Abigail that she wanted to become a doctor.

"She would have to study for years to be a doctor here on Malatha, but maybe she would settle on being a physician's assistant instead," Aaron said.

"I'll talk to Aiden about it tonight after dinner," he continued.

He reached over on the coffee table and picked up the remote. He pressed music and a soft slow ballet began to play. He sipped on his glass of wine and tried to relax, unwinding from his long day at work. He worked constantly without a day off for two months. It was time for a vacation.

"Maybe I'll take Abigail to the mountains, she would love to sightsee," he said to himself as he lay back, closed his eyes, and began to relax.

The house was quiet. Abigail and Amanda were in the kitchen preparing dinner, and Aiden was in the garage working on his hovercar. So, Aaron had the family room to himself and all he wanted to do was relax his eyes.

The music was soft, and Aaron thought about the time he took Aiden skiing in the mountains. Aiden caught on and learned to ski quickly. There wasn't too much of anything that his son couldn't do well. That's why he didn't worry much when Aiden told him that he was going to join the military. Aaron knew he was going to make an excellent soldier.

Aiden walked into the family room and sat down next to his father on the couch. Aaron opened his eyes and looked at Aiden who was holding a tablet in his hand.

"Look at this, dad," he said in a low voice.

He handed Aaron the tablet. It had a picture of an olive-skinned man with black hair and a square-shaped jaw.

Aaron looked at the picture.

"Who is that, son?" he asked strolling through the photos.

"That's Barnabas Drapers. We are investigating him. He is going to try to take some women to Cyprus Five to sell them into sex slavery," Aiden said.

Aaron's eyes widened as he looked at Aiden.

"What?" he asked in surprise.

"He is going to –"

"I heard what you said. Who is dumb enough to try a stunt like that?" Aaron said.

"Apparently, he is," Aiden said as he told his father the whole story.

He told Aaron about Barnabas, his brother, and his ship. Aaron was at a loss for words. He couldn't believe that someone would try such a thing.

"I'm worried dad," Aiden said. "I'm worried about Amanda."

"She isn't telling me anything, but sometimes I think she knows about Barnabas and believes that he is really going to take her and the other women back to Earth," he continued.

"What gives you that idea, son?" Aaron asked.

"Because of the way she asked for some time. One moment she is hot. The next moment she is cold and doesn't want to be bothered. She wouldn't act that way if she didn't think she was going to leave," Aiden said as he buried his head in his hands and began to cry.

Aaron sat up and looked at Aiden.

"Son, look at me. Amanda might have had a hard time adjusting, but she is fine now. I don't think she knows anything about Barnabas. So, don't worry about that. If you want, I'll tell Abigail to keep an eye on her until all of this blows over. But I think you are worrying yourself for nothing. You and Amanda are good for each other, and Amanda is smart. She knows that. I don't think she would throw that away," Aiden looked up at his father and then wiped at his tears.

"I hope so, dad."

"God knows I tried everything in my power to make Amanda happy. And just when I think everything's okay, she does something to make me think the worst."

"She does something?" Aaron asked in surprise. "She does something like what, son?"

"Well, the other day I tried to kiss her. Just a harmless kiss, but she pulled back like I was a stranger. She said that she was cold and tired, but I didn't believe her." Aaron looked at his son.

"Don't read too much into that, son. Amanda loves you and I don't think she would do anything to hurt you."

CHAPTER

Milo Le Grand had just finished up his barbecue. He cooked a variety of meat and sausages for the party he was having tonight. He had planned this party for over a month and tonight was the best night for it because all of his friends had the night off.

Donna had cooked the rest of the food and prepared a big salad to go along with the meat. She had gone to the bakery earlier that day and bought some freshly baked bread and a zubarb red pie, Milo's favorite.

His mother used to make it for him every year on his birthday. Now he has to settle for bakery-made pie because his parents were on Dacia, Malatha's mother planet. Donna was an 'okay' cook, but she couldn't get the hang of making Malatha's pastry. The technique took time and patience that Donna didn't have.

Since Milo and Donna have been married, Milo had done all of the cooking and taking care of the house. Donna wasn't a housewife type. She didn't take care of her mother's house on Earth. So, she wasn't going to take care of Milo's. All she liked to do was shop.

But tonight was different. They were going to have a party with all of their friends. It will give Donna the opportunity to show off their new house. So, she cooked, cleaned, and prepared all day. She thought that she had hidden the fact that she was going away with Barnabas.

Milo didn't have a clue, and she was proud of that. She is just going to leave on the day of the departure. She wasn't even going to give an excuse, because she could come and go as she pleases.

"Milo loves me and trusts me. He would never think I would run away. Until it is too late," she thought.

She helped Milo set the table and they lit the outdoor fire pit. They started the music as well. Donna went upstairs to change her clothes, while Milo sat downstairs and waited for his guests to arrive. Milo looked around the yard to see if anything needed to be done, but everything was great. The table was made of bamboo wood and it had matching bamboo chairs. They had crystal plates and real silverware. Milo's mother gave them the dishes when they moved into their own home.

Bartholomew and Basil, along with their wives Holly and Grace, were the first to arrive. Milo greeted them at the door and showed them to the backyard. Aiden and Amanda rang the doorbell and Milo opened the door.

"Welcome, brother," he said to Aiden as they shook hands.

"Thank you, brother," Aiden said smiling.

"Amanda, you look nice tonight, as always," Milo said.

"Donna is in the kitchen, and Holly and Grace are in the back yard."

Aiden and Amanda walked into the living room. It was large and spacious. It had a silver couch in front of the fireplace and a metallic coffee table in front of it. The floor was made of marble and it had big bay windows looking out into the front yard.

The dining room had a long glass table. It could seat ten people. The floors were also made of marble.

"Your house looks lovely," Amanda said as she looked around.

"Yes, this is really nice. I didn't know that military housing would be this big," Aiden said.

"Yes, it's pretty spacious. We could raise a big family here and still have room for guests," Milo said smiling.

Donna walked into the dining room and shook Aiden's hand.

"I'm glad you two could make it," she said as she hugged Amanda.

"Amanda could you give me a hand in the kitchen?" she asked.

"Sure," Amanda said as she followed Donna into the kitchen.

Donna began putting ice in a large punch bowl.

"Would you give me a hand with this?" she asked.

Amanda went over to help her.

"Have you spoken to Barnabas?" Donna whispered.

Amanda looked around at the kitchen door.

"I have," she answered. Donna smiled.

"Are you ready to go?" Donna asked as her heart began to race.

"Yes, I have to tie up a few loose ends, but I think I am ready," Amanda said as her pulse began to pound. She looked over at the door, afraid that Aiden might be listening.

"You know where to meet us?" Donna asked grinning.

"Yes, and I have a way to get there. Barnabas gave me all the details," Amanda said in a low voice.

"Are you excited? Because I know I am. I can't wait to go," Donna said as she grabbed Amanda by the arm.

"Yes, I'm a little excited, but I'm also afraid. I don't want to get caught. You know they will give us infusement treatment if we get caught," Amanda said.

"I know. Just pray we don't get caught. This is a good plan. I know nothing would go wrong," Donna said.

"Let's take this punch out to my guests before they get suspicious."

CHAPTER

Aiden and Amanda got home a little after midnight. Aiden was still humming the song he heard at Milo's place. It was a new song from his favorite band, The Stargazers. He, Milo, Basil, and Bartholomew love that band. They went to all of their concerts and bought all of their music.

Amanda liked the song too. The music on Malatha was beginning to grow in her. She particularly liked the fast stuff that you could dance to. The house was quiet. Abigail and Aaron had gone to bed.

So, Aiden had turned off the lights as he and Amanda headed upstairs.

Aiden held Amanda's hand as they went up to their bedroom. He was in good spirits. The night went well at Milo's place. They ate dinner and listened to music. There was no conversation about work or Barnabas, or the other women.

That night took all of those things off of Aiden's mind. Tomorrow will be Friday and we would take Barnabas into custody and that will be the end of that, he thought as they walked up the stairs. They walked into their bedroom and Amanda took off her jacket.

"I have to wash off this makeup," she said as she threw her purse on the bed.

Aiden looked at her, walked over, hugged, and kissed her.

"You look lovely tonight," he said. "You always do, that's why I fell in love with you, Amanda. Well, one of the reasons," he said.

Amanda blushed and she returned the kiss to Aiden.

"And you are tall and handsome. That's why I love you," she said laughing.

"Hurry up and get ready for bed," Aiden said as he took off his shirt.

Amanda grabbed her nightgown and robe and ran into the bathroom. Aiden took off his pants and put on his pajama bottoms.

"We should have a barbecue. That meat tasted good," Amanda yelled through the bathroom door.

She washed her face and put toothpaste on her toothbrush.

"Yes, dad would love that. He is the one who usually barbecues. I'll ask him to barbecue on Sunday."

"That will be great," Amanda said as she dried her face.

Aiden buttoned his shirt and went over to the bed to turn the covers down. He picked up Amanda's purse and a white business card fell out of it and onto the blanket. Aiden picked up the card and read it.

His jaw dropped and his blood began to boil.

The business card read:

Barnabas Drapers, Missionary Leader

Written on it as well was his contact information.

Aiden bit his lip, tightened his fist, and punched the pillow.

"I knew it! I knew it all along! She is going to try to go with that bastard Barnabas! How could she do this to me? How could she be so stupid? Can't she tell he is lying? Why would anyone risk their life to take the women back across the galaxy for nothing? She is stupid!"

"I can't believe this. How did she meet him? Every time she went out, my mother was with her."

"My mother, is she in on this too? She lied to me! Could this be true? Barnabas had her fooled as well. She is going to get caught and they are going to take her away from me and my mother is going to be put to death!"

"Oh, my god! Could this be happening?" Aiden said in a low voice as his stomach began to hurt. He rubbed his hand through his hair, took off his pajamas, and put his clothes back on.

"Why does she want to do this? I did everything in my power to make her happy!" he said through clenched teeth.

He bent over and held his stomach as if he had just got kicked in it.

"I have to get some air. It feels like I'm suffocating," he said as his face turned red.

He put the card in his pocket and headed for the door. Amanda came out of the bathroom and to her surprise, Aiden wasn't dressed yet.

"Aiden, you are not dressed for bed yet," she said.

Aiden looked at her and steam came out of his ears.

"I want to go to The Stargazers' concert. I think that they are a good band," Amanda said as she crawled into bed.

"I'm beginning to love the music here. At first, it sounded strange to me because it was new, but now it's fun and wild. I really like it a lot," she continued.

"I like everything about Malatha: the food, the beaches, and the amusement park. I just love it here, Aiden."

"I really do," Amanda said excitedly as she grinned at Aiden.

"*Do you*, Amanda?"

"Do you really want to go to a concert? Because we could go out on Friday at eight o'clock. I can call and get tickets and we could go by then, Amanda," Aiden said as he looked at his wife intensely.

Amanda thought about Friday. Then she thought about Barnabas and the time of the departure. She couldn't go to a concert on Friday or any other Friday. She was going home and that made her heart drop.

CHAPTER

36

Aiden waited for Amanda to respond, but she just sat there as if she was in deep thought. He sat on the bed, his blood still boiling, so he began to put on his shoes.

"I talked to Abigail the other day and she said it would be a good idea for me to take cooking classes at the Civics Center. The first class starts on Friday evening at eight," Amanda said.

Aiden looked at Amanda who looked at him smiling innocently.

"How stupid does she think I am? The classes start at the same time Barnabas is supposed to depart," he thought to himself. His muscles quivered and his heart pounded as if it was going to jump out of his chest. He stood up and glared at Amanda.

"We both think I should take cooking classes so I could learn how to make Malatha dishes."

Aiden's head felt as if it was going to explode. He walked over to Amanda.

"Why do you want to take the classes in the evening? They have classes during the day and on Monday," Aiden asked through clenched teeth.

Amanda jerked her head back.

"I thought if I go in the evening, I could be here to help Abigail with the house chores," she said thinking fast as her pulse raced.

Aiden tried hard to control himself. He held on tight to every muscle in his body, but the rage inside of him was also fighting hard to rise to the surface and boil over. He pulled at his collar as heat rushed through his body. He closes his eyes and beads of sweat popped out of his forehead. He opened his eyes and glared at Amanda.

"Whose idea was it for you to take the cooking classes anyway?!" he snapped.

Amanda put her hand over her lips and squeezed her eyes shut. She began to tremble. She didn't want to make Aiden angry because he might not let her take the cooking class. Then she wouldn't have an excuse to leave the house to meet Barnabas on Friday. She rose up on her knees as if she was pleading with Aiden and looked sadly at him.

"It was your mother's idea. She thought that I should get out more," she said softly.

Aiden began to pace in the middle of the floor. He stopped and shook his fist at Amanda.

"Don't I take you out?!"

"I take you to every place you want to go!" he shouted to the top of his voice.

Amanda's heart dropped. She couldn't believe that Aiden was acting this way. She had never seen him so irate before. She didn't know what to do. She looked at him through tears in her eyes.

"I know, but it's just an hour of cooking class. I would be back home before you know it," she whispered.

Aiden looked at Amanda and shook his head.

How dare she try to make me feel sorry for her? He thought.

"You don't want to take a cooking class! You just want to go out by yourself!" he shouted, losing control.

He put his hand on his head, went over to the chest of drawers, and kicked it.

"Why?"

"Why?!" He repeated.

"Tell me the truth!" Amanda couldn't hold it in any longer. Her blood had begun to boil and her nostrils flared.

"I am telling you the truth!" she shouted.

"I just want to take a cooking class so I can meet more people and state active! If I stay in this house much longer, I'm going to die!" she continued.

Aaron woke up from all of the shouting and shook Abigail. He thought he heard a loud crash. They jumped out of the bed, grabbed their robes, ran out of their bedroom, and rushed down the hall to Aiden's room.

Aaron opened the door and stormed in. Aiden was standing in Amanda's face, shaking his fist.

"What's wrong, Amanda? Being here in these comforts isn't enough for you?! Don't you have friends? What's wrong with Holly and Grace? Aren't they enough for you!" Aiden shouted.

Amanda shut her eyes and pushed Aiden with her chest.

"What are you going to do? Hit me? Go ahead!"

"You took me from my planet, and you brought me here! You made me live with you and you keep me caged up in this house! Now you say that I can't take a cooking class?!"

"Hit me! Go ahead hit me!" she cried. "I knew it was coming sooner or later!" Amanda cried louder.

Aiden's eyes widened. He frowned his face until it turned red. He tightened his fist, but with all of his might, he held back. He wanted to hit Amanda, but he was too much of a gentleman, and he loved her too much.

He didn't bring her there to a bruise her. He inhaled and held his breath, but his rage was still there. He had to get some air and calm down. He had to think about what he was going to do next.

"I'm not going to hit you. That's what you want me to do because it would justify what you want to do," he said calmly.

Amanda sat back down on the bed and began to cry.

"But go ahead, Amanda. Go to your cooking class."

Aiden looked down at her and put his hand on his chest.

"All I ever tried to do was love you. But you are too selfish and selfcentered to see that. Go to your cooking class. I don't care what happens to you anymore. I did everything in my power to make you happy, but I see that it isn't good enough for you. You could go to the moon for all I care."

"All right, that's enough!" Aaron shouted as he grabbed Aiden by the arm.

"That's enough both of you!" he said firmly.

"Aiden, go downstairs. I want to talk to you," Aiden looked at Aaron.

"It's alright, dad. I'm fine. It's nothing I can't handle," Aiden said. Aaron looked at him wide-eyed.

"Oh, you handled this just fine."

Abigail came inside the room and put her hand on Aiden's shoulder.

"Are you okay, son?" she asked.

Aiden snatched his arm away. Abigail's mouth dropped. Aaron pushed Aiden to the door.

"Let's go downstairs! I'm not telling you again!" he snapped.

Aiden went out into the hall but then he turned and came back to the room.

"I didn't take you from your home planet. What happened to you wasn't my –"

Aaron grabbed him and pushed him outside towards the hall.

CHAPTER

37

Aiden and Aaron went downstairs. Aiden zipped up his jacket and headed for the front door. Aaron followed behind him.

"Where are you going at this time of night?" Aaron asked angrily.

"I have to get some air," Aiden said as the rage inside of him lingered in his soul.

"Come into the family room," Aaron said firmly. "I want to talk to you."

Aiden went into the family room and sat down on the couch. Aaron walked into the room and closed the door behind him.

"What's wrong with you, Aiden? You don't talk to a lady like that. I taught you better than that. You never heard me and your mother argue. What got into you?"

"I saw how you snatched away from your mother. Did things go that bad tonight you had to wake up the whole neighborhood?"

Aiden looked at his father and rolled his eyes. He inhaled, trying to calm his pulse, but all he could hear were Amanda words,

"You took me from my home planet and brought me here!"

He wanted to go upstairs and slap Amanda's face until she saw that Barnabas was nothing but a liar.

"Do you hear me, son?" Aaron snapped.

Aiden looked at his father.

"Yes, I hear you," he finally said.

"Then why are you and Amanda fighting?" Aaron asked.

"I tried daddy. I did everything in my power to make Amanda safe and happy, but now they are going to take her away from me on Friday, and there's nothing I can do!"

"Take her away? Who is going to take her away?" Aaron said confused.

Aiden pulled the card out of his pocket and showed it to his father.

"You know Barnabas, that man I told you about the other day? He is going to kidnap some women and take them to Cyprus Five to sell them into sex slavery."

"Yes," Aaron said looking at the card.

"Well, Amanda had been talking to him. She wants to go. She asked me if she could go to some cooking class at the Civics Center at the same time that Barnabas was supposed to leave."

Aaron's eyes widened and his heart began to pound out of his chest.

"Are you sure she is trying to go with him? How did she get in contact with a person like that?" he asked as he sat down the couch.

"I don't know, but I think mom helped her. Mom told me that Amanda didn't meet anyone when she went out, but she met Barnabas."

"Don't say that, son. Your mother wouldn't do anything to break the law intentionally. She wouldn't hurt you like that. There has to be another explanation."

Aiden stood up.

"Then what could it be? I can't think of another explanation. All I know is Amanda wants to go with Barnabas and my mother is helping her."

"Don't say that son, because it's not true. Abigail wouldn't do anything like that."

"We opened up our home to Amanda and I tried to make her welcome. Abigail bent over backwards trying to help her adjust to life here on Malatha. She wouldn't try to help her escape. She wouldn't do that. There has to be another reason why Amanda has that card."

"Maybe she found it, or it could have been lying on a table or a counter at one of the stores they went to, but I don't think Abigail helped her get it. Before you accuse your mother, let's ask her if she knows how Amanda got the card."

Aaron said as he swallowed the lump in his throat. He stood up, went out into the living room, and walked to the bottom of the stairs.

"Abigail!" he called.

She came downstairs and Aaron led her to the family room. Abigail's pulse raced as she saw the seriousness on Aaron's face.

"Sit down, Abigail," Aaron said as he motioned to the armchair by the couch.

"Why? What happened?" Abigail asked with a shaky voice.

"Sit down!" Aaron said firmly.

"Abigail, we have been married for over thirty years. We've been through a lot together. You brought my only child into this world," Aaron said as he looked into Abigail's eyes.

"Yes," she said as she looked at Aiden. "What is wrong?" she asked again.

"When you and Amanda went out, who did she meet with?" Abigail looked confused.

"We went out several times," she said.

"Did Amanda meet with anyone at any of those times?"

Abigail thought for a moment then it came back to her – the time when they were at the market.

"Yes, once when we were at the market," she said. "Amanda met with two women she knew from the ship." Aaron looked at Aiden.

"How long did they talk?" Aiden asked as the rage rose up inside of him.

"They talked for about ten minutes," Abigail said as her body shook. "Why didn't you tell me that before, mom?" Aiden cried. "I didn't think anything of it. I thought it was harmless."

Aiden told Abigail everything about Barnabas and Amanda.

"Oh, my god! She asked me if she could take the cooking class! I thought that it would be harmless!" Aaron walked over to Abigail and hugged her.

"What are you going to do now?" Aaron asked.

"I don't know," Aiden said. "But I have to think of something."

Amanda sat on the bed and cried.

"Why is Aiden so angry?" she said.

"I can't wait until Friday. I have to get out of here. This is crazy."

She got up and began to pace, but then she saw Aiden's picture on the chest of drawers, and her heart fluttered because she loved him. No matter how much she tried to fool herself, she knew that she loved Aiden with all of her heart. She wiped off the tears in her eyes.

"I have to go. I have to see my grandmother. You are not in love. You don't love Aiden," she said over and over.

She crawled back in bed, but her chest hurt. She knew that she did love Aiden, because he was the first guy to ever kiss her.

CHAPTER

38

Aiden sat and stared at the blank computer screen. He squinted to see the computer through puffy eyes. His chest ached and his throat was painful and scratchy. He had to write a report on the latest activities of Barnabas Drapers for Col. Galveston's files.

Aiden tried to dictate the report into his microphone, but he was at a loss for words. So, he decided to type it. His mind worked best when he typed out his report. Aiden was going to meet with Bartholomew later for lunch, but he just wanted to be alone.

He didn't know what to do about Amanda. Today was Friday and tonight was the night that they were going to take Barnabas into custody.

Since he met Amanda, he wanted her to love him for who he was. He didn't want to feel like her love was forced or that she was frightened into loving him. Aiden wanted her to genuinely love him. Like the women in those corny magazines his mother read.

He wanted true love. That's why he didn't tell Amanda about Barnabas. He wanted her to choose him over her grandmother, her brother, and Earth.

Aiden wanted to be truly loved by another female companion. He wanted what his father was lucky enough to have. A female who truly loved him and was willing to spend the rest of her life with him, without fear, force, or need. Aiden tried to type his report, but his fingers hurt. All he wanted to do was cry and feel sorry for himself.

He sat at the computer thinking about the time he had with Amanda, and how wonderful it was to talk to her and hear about her wants and desires. Even though they were wants for a planet on the other side of the galaxy.

Aiden wanted to heal her pain and make her feel loved and accepted. He wanted her to forget about how she got there and accept that she was there, but all he got was pain. Amanda couldn't forget. She wouldn't even try. He was a fool to think that there was love at first sight. Maybe you can't love your captive and it was silly of him to think he could, he thought.

Aiden stood up, walked over to the window, and watched the cadets do their drills. He thought about last night. He stayed in the family room for the rest of the night. Then he got up, before everyone else, got dressed, and left early.

He drove to his favorite spot by the lake in the woods and thought about what he was going to do after tonight. He thought that he would put in a transfer and go to Dacia, and become a fighter pilot.

"Fighter pilots travel. They don't stay in one place. That's just what I need," Aiden thought.

Aiden went back to his office desk and sat down. He hit at the pain in his chest and swallowed the lump in his throat. He stared at the blank computer screen.

"I was just fooling myself thinking I could be happy," he said.

Bartholomew was excited because he was invited to go and participate in the arrest of Barnabas. He couldn't wait until tonight so he could look at a criminal like Barnabas in the face. He was going to eat a big lunch with his best pal Aiden, and after he arrests Barnabas tonight, he was going to eat another big dinner with Holly.

He was glad that Holly wasn't on the list of names who were trying to escape. Holly truly loved him. He felt lucky. He went into the office and sat down in the chair in front of Aiden's desk. He looked at Aiden's puffy eyes and red face.

"Woah! Man, you look terrible. What happened?" Bartholomew asked, concerned for his friend.

Aiden looked at him and put his head on his desk.

"I didn't get much sleep last night," he said with tears in his eyes.

Bartholomew's eyes widened. He had never seen Aiden cry before. "Woah. What's wrong, man?" he asked. "Why the tears?"

Aiden lay back on his seat and wiped at his eyes.

"It's Amanda. She is one of those women who are going to get caught tonight."

Bartholomew's heart dropped and he forced himself to hear Aiden better.

"What? Are you sure?!" he shouted.

Aiden looked at him.

"I'm sure. She is at home as we speak, getting ready to go."

Bartholomew stood up.

"Man, how do you know?"

Aiden got up, walked to the door, looked outside, and then he closed it back.

"I found Barnabas' business card in her purse. She had been talking to him," he said as tears ran down his face.

Bartholomew walked over to Aiden and put his hand on his shoulder.

"Ah, man, you have to stop her! Don't let her go down like that."

Aiden looked down on the floor.

"I want to, but I want her to choose me not because she has to, but because she wants to."

Bartholomew frowned. He couldn't believe he heard his friend say that.

"Come on, Aiden. She loves you, man! I can see it in her eyes! She did choose you!"

Aiden shook his head and walked back over to his desk.

"No, she didn't choose me. I chose her. I signed that contract. I forced her to come to my home and forced her to love me!" "I chose her!" Aiden said pointing to his chest.

Bartholomew threw his hands up.

"Don't think that way. You are the guy. You are supposed to choose her and you are a fool if you think she doesn't love you! So, get up, go home, and stop her, before it's too late!" Bartholomew said.

Aiden sat down and turned toward his computer as if he were to type something.

"I told my mother to let her go. Let her do whatever her heart tells her to do. I'm tired of fighting with her. Love isn't supposed to hurt," he said.

Bartholomew walked over to Aiden and shook his head.

"Love does hurt and true love is worth fighting for. If you truly love Amanda, you will fight for her. You wouldn't let her go down like that. If De Ivory gives her infusement treatment, she would never be the same!" "You have to save her, man! Come on, get up!" Aiden looked at Bartholomew.

"You don't understand. Ever since they said that they were going to bring those women here, I had it in my mind that I was going to get myself a wife. A nice girl who would love me, trust me, and let me take care of her. But Amanda doesn't trust me, and she definitely doesn't need me to take care of her. I don't think she loves me," Aiden said sobbing.

Bartholomew's heart went out for Aiden. He didn't know how to convince his friend to go and stop Amanda, but he was going to stop this from happening even if he had to stop her himself.

"Yes, she loves you. You are making a big mistake," he said sadly.

CHAPTER

Abigail walked passed Aiden and Amanda's bedroom door. She stopped and listened in on Amanda, but the room was quiet. She didn't hear Amanda moving around in her room. It was one o'clock and Amanda didn't come out of her room all day.

Abigail went downstairs to the kitchen and made herself a cup of coffee. She sat up at the kitchen island and began to read the news on her tablet. She wanted to talk to Amanda and tell her that the family loved her. That she loved her. And she should really think about that.

She wanted to go to Amanda's room and tell her what was on her mind, but Aiden had pleaded with her and asked her to let Amanda make up her mind to stay with them. So, she didn't disturb Amanda. She decided to wait until Amanda came downstairs to talk to her.

She sipped on her coffee and thought about what she was going to say, but she didn't quite know what she wanted to say. She only knew that she wasn't going to let Amanda leave the house tonight even if she had to physically restrain her herself.

She wasn't going to let Amanda get into any trouble, and she wasn't going to let De Ivory give her infusement treatment. The phone rang and Abigail went over to the panel on the wall to accept the call. Aaron came on the screen. He looked at Abigail, who looked worried and tired.

"How are you doing, honey?" he asked with concern in his eyes.

"I'm doing better than expected," Abigail said rubbing her hands on her apron.

"What is Amanda doing?" Aaron asked, afraid that Amanda was up and getting ready to leave.

He wanted to stay at home from work that day, but Aiden begged him to go to work. So, he went, but he thought about Amanda all day. Abigail looked toward the doorway at the stairs.

"She didn't come out of her room all day. I don't know what to do. You know I just can't let her go anywhere," Abigail said.

"No, don't let her go anywhere. I don't care what Aiden says. Keep her there for as long as you can. And I will be home at around three. I would think of something, but until then, keep an eye on her," Aaron said as his pulse raced and his body tensed up.

He loved Amanda too, and he knew that Aiden still loved her. He didn't want Aiden to regret not trying to stop Amanda from going to meet Barnabas.

"I have to go. I'll see you later," he said.

Abigail ended the call and went back to the kitchen island and drank her coffee. She thought she heard Amanda moving around upstairs, but when she went to look, there was no one. So, she got up and moved to the living room so she could see Amanda when she came downstairs. She got her tablet, brought up one of her novels, and began to read while waiting for Amanda to come down.

Amanda lay in bed with the covers over her head all day. She was still hurt over the fight she had with Aiden last night. She didn't know why Aiden was so upset, but what he said was true. He did do everything in his power to make her happy. And she was selfish and self-centered.

Every day they spent together, she thought of no one but herself. She loved Aiden and she didn't want to lose him. She loved her grandmother too. She had to really think hard about what she wanted to do. She wanted to go back to Earth and see her brother and her grandmother, but she wanted to stay with Aiden too.

When she thought of Aiden, her heart banged on the walls of her chest, her stomach tied up in knots, and her knees got weak. She had never felt that way for anyone before and she loved it. She didn't ever want to lose that feeling, but then she thought of her grandmother and Steve. She didn't know what happened to them and she would hate herself if she didn't try to find out.

She knew that tonight was the night that she had to meet Barnabas, but instead of feeling excited, she felt like a traitor. She felt like she was really letting Aiden down. She couldn't get his face out of her mind and her heart longed to be with him. She dragged herself out of bed and looked at the clock. It was 1:30 and she had to get ready.

After Amanda got dressed, she went downstairs to get a bite to eat. She went into the living room and to her surprise, Abigail was sitting in her armchair in the living room. She was waiting for her.

"Amanda, can I talk to you for a minute?" Abigail asked as Amanda walked into the living room.

She smiled and sat down. She always gave Abigail and Aaron a little smile to show her appreciation.

"Sure, Abigail," she said.

"Amanda, you know that Aaron and I have grown to love you as our own daughter. And we don't want anything to happen to you. We want you to know that you have a home right here with us for as long as you live."

Amanda shook her head and listened carefully to what Abigail had to say.

"Amanda you know that Aiden loves you more than anything or anyone in the world, and he would give his life for you. And that's something you should cherish. Not too many people get that kind of love from anyone in a lifetime. It will be a real shame for you to throw something like that away."

"So, you should really think about what you are doing. I mean really think about the life you have here with us," Abigail said.

Amanda looked at Abigail and she thought about what she said. Her heart fluttered and she wanted to burst into tears because she knew that her new family loved her as much as her grandmother and Steve did. She would give her life for Aiden too.

CHAPTER

Aiden, Bartholomew, and Col. Galveston were dressed as mechanics wearing long tight jumpsuits, black boots, and black utility belts. They were pretending to work on an old cargo ship at Ship Dock 6.

The dock was across the shipyard from Ship Dock 7, where Barnabas Drapers' ship was. Lieut. De Grey, Basil, and Milo were stationed at Ship Dock 8. They were also wearing mechanic uniforms and waiting for Barnabas.

The port was dark and foggy. All of the workers had gone home for the night. The ship port was large, and it housed over a hundred different types of cargo ships. It wasn't a port for passenger ships. It was a port for ships that hauled cargo fuel and other hazardous materials.

Aiden looked around the shipyard; it was quiet and eerie. The ground was large and dusty. The moon shined full and bright. It cast a gloomy light over the yard. The air was cool, giving Aiden a doleful chill.

He shivered, trying to shake the depressed feeling off of him. It was 7:45 and some of the women had begun to show up. Aiden's heart pounded out of his chest as he thought that Amanda would show up. "What am I going to tell Col. Galveston?" he thought.

"Don't make a move until you see Barnabas," Col. Galveston said to De Grey through his wrist band.

Bartholomew looked at Aiden, who looked like he had just lost his best friend.

"You still have time go. Get out of here and find Amanda before it's too late," he whispered.

Aiden looked down at the ground.

"No man, I have to see if she loves me or if she is just playing games."

Some more women showed up and then began to gather by the ship's entrance.

"This doesn't make any sense," Col. Galveston said.

"If Barnabas doesn't want to get caught, why would he let the women gather out here? Should we arrest them now?" De Grey asked.

"No, not just yet. Let's wait a little longer."

"How many women do you think are out there?" Col. Galveston asked De Grey.

"I count about sixty, sir," De Grey answered.

Barnabas raised the door to the ship and stepped out with a tablet in his hand.

"Gather around, women," he said as he began calling out their names.

More women showed up as Barnabas read off their names. He started to let them board the ship.

"Should we arrest them now?" De Grey asked again.

"No, let them go all the way to the ship," Galveston said.

Cyr had the women filing into the ship two by two.

Col. Galveston watched in disgust as they made their way into the ship.

"Alright, ladies. No need to push. Just hurry up. We have to depart at eight o'clock," Cyr said.

Aiden watched silently, looking at each woman as she got on the ship, but he didn't see Amanda. Just as they were finished loading the women on the ship, three more women ran over to Cyr to get on the ship. It was Hope, Faith, and Donna.

Donna's face glowed in the moonlight. Aiden, Bartholomew, Basil, and Milo recognized her instantly. Milo began to shout out her name and ran over to her, but De Grey and Basil held him back. De Grey put his hand over his mouth.

Aiden was frightened that Amanda was going to show up. The three women boarded the ship. Cyr looked around for more.

"We will wait here for ten minutes, then we will close the door and depart," Barnabas said.

Col. Galveston gave the go signal and Bartholomew, Aiden, Basil, and De Grey grabbed their rifles and ran over to Ship Dock 7 to arrest Barnabas and the women. De Grey grabbed Cyr and threw him down to the ground, putting handcuffs on him.

Col. Galveston, Aiden, and Bartholomew went inside the ship. The women started to scream. Drogo tried to run in the engine room, but Aiden caught him and threw him up against the wall.

"You are under arrest! You son of a bitch!" he yelled.

Barnabas was on the bridge and Col. Galveston made his way there. The door opened and Col. Galveston stepped into the bridge with his phaser ready. Barnabas saw Col. Galveston step inside the bridge.

He ran over to his case of rifles, but Galveston cut him off.

"It's over, Barnabas!" Galveston said as he grabbed him and threw him to the floor. Galveston put his knee in Barnabas' back and handcuffed him.

"How did you know?!" Barnabas yelled.

"You can't fool the government," Galveston said.

Barnabas, Cyr, and Drogo had handcuffs on them as they sat on the cold ground. Bartholomew and Basil had gathered up all of the women. Col. Galveston had Barnabas' tablet with his list of names on it. They gathered the women, calling them by name and put them on a bus to take them to the infusement treatment center.

Milo ran over and grabbed Donna, who was on the bus with the other women.

"Why Donna? Why?!" he yelled.

Aiden and Bartholomew grabbed him and dragged him away. Col. Galveston walked over to Barnabas.

"You destroyed a lot of lives tonight. Why would you want to do something like this?" Galveston asked.

Barnabas looked at him and spat on the ground.

"For the money," he said smiling.

Drogo looked up at Barnabas.

"What is going to happen to us now?"

"Don't worry, Drogo. Everything will be just fine," Barnabas said.

Col. Galveston walked over to Bartholomew and Aiden.

"All of the women showed up except five. Keep a lookout for them while we haul the others in. Wait here another hour. If they don't show up, perhaps they changed their mind. We won't bother them. If they do show up, haul them to the infusement treatment center," Galveston said.

CHAPTER

Amanda was in her room, getting ready to go meet Barnabas. She put on a comfortable dress and some thick tights because the women on Malatha didn't wear pants.

"What would I do for a pair of blue jeans right now?" Amanda said.

She got a big purse and packed it with more dresses and tights, and some toiletries. She looked at the clock – it was six o'clock. It would take her an hour to make it to the cargo shipyard. Amanda tried hard to remember her grandmother and why she was going home, but what Abigail said to her lingered in her mind.

"Aiden loves you more than anything in the world."

Amanda's heart fluttered and her stomach felt uneasy because she loved Aiden too. She thought about how he looked at her and how he made her feel like a queen when they were together. She thought about the time he took her to the beach and the amusement park.

"Aiden would give his life for you," Abigail said.

"Some people don't get that kind of love in a lifetime. Not even on Earth," Amanda said.

She sat on the bed.

"What if they won't let me see my grandmother when I get there? What if there isn't an Earth anymore?" she thought.

She walked over to the window and looked out.

"What if we get caught? Aiden would never forgive me, and I would let Abigail and Aaron down. The two people who opened their home to me and treated me like a daughter."

"My grandmother would tell me to stay with Aiden, where I will be safe. And she would try her best to take care of Steve. Steve is a big boy now; he could handle himself," she said as tears flowed down her face.

"I'm going to stay here where I am safe, and I know nothing bad will happen to me if I obey the laws."

"I love you grandmother, and I know you love me. If I could, I would go back, but this isn't the way. Maybe one day Aiden will be able to take me to Earth and then I will see you again."

Amanda cried with her eyes closed as she imagined her grandmother sitting in her recliner.

"Steve, you be sweet and take care of your grandmother. One day I will see you again. I promise."

She walked back to her bed, emptied out her purse, and changed her clothes.

"I have to show Aiden that I love him and that I'm sorry for the attitude that I had in the past."

She went downstairs and looked for Abigail. Abigail was sitting in the family room watching a movie on the viewing screen. Amanda came into the family room and walked up to Abigail.

"Abigail, I thought about what you said, and I thank you for allowing me to stay here with you and Aaron. I know that Aiden loves me more than anything and I love him with all of my heart. I don't want to do anything to hurt him anymore. I want to stay here and have children, go back to school, and build my life here in Surrok with Aiden, and you and Aaron."

Abigail's heart overflowed with joy. She clapped her hands together, jumped up, and hugged Amanda. Amanda smiled with tears rolling down her cheek.

"I'm sorry for the things I said the other night. I didn't mean them. I know it's not Aiden's fault I'm here."

Abigail looked at her and smiled.

"That's okay, babe. You both said things you didn't mean," she said as she hugged Amanda again.

"I want to do something special for Aiden. To show him how much I love him," Amanda said smiling. "I want to cook his favorite dessert." Abigail looked at her and smiled.

"A molten pudding? He would love that," Abigail said.

"Let's get started before he comes home. He said that he was going to work late, but he will be surprised when he comes home," Abigail said.

The two women ran around the kitchen and gathered all of the ingredients for the molten pudding. Amanda cut up all of the berries and Abigail made the sauce. Aaron came home from work and walked through the front door.

He heard Abigail and Amanda laughing in the kitchen. He hurried into the kitchen and to his surprise, Amanda was there, making a molten pudding.

"Mmm! What smells so good in here?" he asked smiling.

"Oh, honey! Amanda is making a molten pudding to surprise Aiden when he comes home," Abigail said.

"Oh, really? So is everything alright?" Aaron asked looking at Abigail.

"Everything's fine. We are not going anywhere," Abigail said as she winked her eye at Aaron.

"I want to make Aiden a special dessert to show him how much I love him," Amanda said.

"Well ladies, let me get out of your way," Aaron said smiling.

CHAPTER

42

Aiden and Bartholomew waited at the ship port for over an hour, but the other women didn't show up. Aiden's stomach was in knots. He was nervous that Amanda was going to show up. He sat on the ground by Ship Dock 6, waiting nervously for her.

"Do you think she is going to show up?" Bartholomew asked as he paced back and forth.

"I don't know. It's a quarter to ten. If she was going to show up, she would have been here by now," Aiden said frustrated. He rubbed his hand through his hair and checked his rifle.

"Are you sure she was going to come? Maybe she just found that card and held onto it, but she wasn't intending to show up. She probably didn't even talk to Barnabas," Bartholomew said, trying to reassure his friend.

Aiden thought for a minute. He didn't know what to think about Amanda. Did she change her mind or did she get lost and couldn't find her way to the shipyard? Or maybe Bartholomew was right? Perhaps she didn't intend to come in the first place.

"Maybe you were right Bartholomew. I probably jumped into conclusions when I found that card. I should have talked to Amanda before I accused her," Aiden said.

"Well, we should head back to the detention center and tell Col. Galveston that the other five women didn't show up," Bartholomew said.

Deep in Aiden's heart, he was relieved that Amanda didn't show up. He said a little prayer and thanked God. They got up and gathered their things, and went to the criminal detention center where Col. Galveston took Barnabas and the seventy women who were caught. De Ivory was there, getting the paperwork ready for the women to have infusement treatment.

It was supposed to start first thing in the morning, but first, he had to interview each and every one of the women and get a statement from them. He called each woman one by one in the interrogation room to ask them why they were persuaded into going with Barnabas.

Some women begged and cried not to get infusement treatment, but De Ivory told them that that was the punishment for disobeying the laws.

"The laws were given and explained to you for your own safety and for the good of the society, and they weren't meant to be broken," De Ivory said.

He had gathered all of the information on the women and called their husbands. The men were angry and confused. They didn't know what was going on. They tried to speak on behalf of their wives, but De Ivory simply said that the law was broken and the women had to be punished.

De Ivory asked the men to come to the infusement treatment center to see their wives one last time before the treatment. Each woman was given thirty minutes with her husband. Col. Galveston was in the interrogation room with Barnabas.

Barnabas couldn't understand how a perfect plan like his backfired. He had thought carefully about the plan and was very careful not to tip off the authorities, but he didn't understand how Galveston found out.

At first, he wasn't going to say anything until he got himself a lawyer, but he thought about it and decided to cooperate for Drogo's sake. Maybe if he confesses, they will go easy on his little brother. Drogo was only twenty-four. He had his whole life ahead of him.

It was too late for Barnabas who was pushing forty and who was nothing but a common criminal. But Drogo had time to change and make something out of his life. So, he made a deal with Galveston that he will cooperate and confess everything so that Drogo could go free after a few years.

Col. Galveston agreed, and Barnabas and Cyr took the heat. Drogo got three years in the criminal detention center. He was frightened and confused. He didn't want Barnabas to take the heat all by himself, but Barnabas talked to him and told him that when he was free, he could have his ship and the little money he had saved. Barnabas told him to leave Surrok and never look back.

Milo was in the waiting room, sitting on the couch with his head in his hands. Aiden and Bartholomew had come in and sat down beside him. His eyes were puffy and his face was red from crying. He couldn't understand why Donna had decided to throw away everything they had.

He thought that he had given her a nice life. He had just purchased a nice home and had given Donna everything she could ever want.

"I don't get it! Why did she have to do this to me?!" he cried.

Aiden put his hand on Milo's shoulder.

His heart went out for him because he knew how he felt about Amanda. He didn't know what he would have done if Amanda would have shown up.

"She didn't try to hurt you. She thought she was going back to Earth. Barnabas had got to her and she listened to him," Aiden said, trying to comfort his friend.

"Yeah, man. She didn't try to hurt you," Bartholomew said.

"But, look at your wives! They didn't try to go with Barnabas, because they love you," Milo said as he got up and started to pace.

Aiden looked at Bartholomew. He wondered if Amanda truly loved him the way that Milo thought.

"Donna loves you too, and don't ever think she didn't," Aiden said.

De Ivory came into the room.

"Lieutenant Le Grand. Donna is ready to see you now. She is scheduled for infusement treatment at one o'clock in the afternoon tomorrow. And, she will be in recovery for about three months."

CHAPTER

Tears flowed down Donna's face like a waterfall. She didn't understand how Barnabas got caught. She begged De Ivory to let her go home, but he told her that she had to be sentenced for breaking the law. De Ivory told her that Milo was in the waiting area, waiting to see her and that he deserved an explanation for her actions.

Donna's heart jumped to her throat and she shook violently because she didn't want Milo to see her like that. She tried to hold back the tears that flowed down her face.

Milo's blood was boiling. All he wanted was an explanation. He didn't want anything else from Donna.

"I opened up my heart to her and tried to give her a good life, but this is my pay!" he said to De Ivory as he walked down the hall to the holding room.

"Just listen to her and allow her to explain herself to you. She owes you that much," De Ivory said.

Milo shook his head yes and tightened his fist. He didn't know how he was going to react when he saw Donna.

'Keep your cool. Don't show her you are upset," he thought.

De Ivory and Milo walked to the door. Milo looked through the window of the door at Donna who was sitting at the table with her head in her hands. She was crying.

Milo's heart went out for her even though she tried to get away and go back to Earth, and leave him. He still loved her.

"She wasn't trying to hurt me. It wasn't personal," he thought. He looked through the window at her round face, her medium complexion, her soft lips, and brown eyes. He remembered why he loved her so much.

De Ivory opened the door and Milo stepped inside the room. Donna jumped up and ran over to him, throwing her arms around his neck.

"Oh, Milo. Please forgive me! I just wanted to go home and see my family! Barnabas told me that he was going to take me home and I believed him! I didn't think about how much it was going to hurt you!" she cried.

Milo grabbed her arm and pulled her off of him. His heart was in his throat as waves of tears filled his eyes.

"Look at me, Donna," he said trying to choke back the emotion building up inside of him.

"You are in trouble and I can't help you now. Why didn't you just come to me and tell me your feelings?"

Donna looked at him and sobbed.

"I'm sorry. I knew you wouldn't let me go. So, I snuck away," she said as she put her head in her hands and cried.

"De Ivory is going to give you infusement treatment and after that, I don't know what is going to happen to you."

"What are you saying, Milo? Are you going to leave me? Please don't leave me?" She cried.

Tears flowed down Milo's cheeks as he looked at Donna.

"I don't know what I'm going to do. I have to think and straighten things out. I don't know how you will be after the treatment." "I'll be fine. You'll see. I will beat this. I'll be the same, Milo." Donna cried. Milo looked at her.

"I hope so Donna, for your sake."

"Please tell me that you will be here when the treatment is over?"

"I will Donna. I'll be here. I won't let you go through that by yourself."

He hugged her and kissed her on the cheek.

"You be brave and don't cry anymore. I'll be right here when it's over." He looked at Donna one last time and then he walked out of the room. Two doctors walked into the room, took Donna, and accompanied her to the treatment room. Donna's legs gave in and she slumped to the floor.

They picked her up and walked her slowly to the room.

It seemed like days passed since Donna went into the treatment room. Milo sat in the waiting area trying to think of more pleasant things, but his body shook uncontrollably and waves moved through his stomach.

He couldn't help but think about how Donna was going to be after the treatment.

De Ivory came into the room.

"Milo," He said softly.

"Donna is in recovery. You can go see her now."

Milo jumped up and walked slowly down the hall to Donna's room. His heart pounded out of his chest and his body trembled all over. He opened the door and walked inside Donna's room. She was lying in bed with the covers up to her head. Milo walked up to the bed and she opened her eyes.

"Hi, Donna," Milo said with tears in his eyes.

Donna looked at him and smiled. She tried to speak, but her speech was slurred.

"Don't try to speak, Donna. Try to get some rest," Milo said as he bent over and kissed her.

"My head feels like it's spinning," Donna said through slurred speech.

"Shhh, quiet now," Milo said. "Don't try to speak."

De Ivory came into the room and looked at Donna.

"Donna, how do you feel?" he said smiling as he put his hand on her foot.

Donna shook her head.

"Okay," she said.

"Get some sleep now," De Ivory said. He then turned to Milo.

"The treatment went well. Donna didn't try to resist. She has a strong will. I think she will make a full recovery. She won't be a hundred percent well, but she would be like ninety-eight percent. You two could still have a good life together," De Ivory said.

Milo smiled as he looked at Donna.

"I hope so. It doesn't seem right to just leave her."

"No, I think she will be fine," De Ivory said. "After a couple of months, you could go on with your lives," he continued.

Milo looked at Donna and his heart sang with joy.

CHAPTER

It was a quarter to twelve when Aiden got home. He turned off the engine to his car and looked at the living room window. The lights were still on and it looked like everyone was still up. He didn't know what became of Amanda.

She didn't show up at the ship port, but her name was on the list of names who were supposed to go with Barnabas. De Ivory had said that he was going to overlook the women who didn't show up because they changed their minds and didn't break any law.

Aiden was happy that Amanda didn't get into any trouble, but he had to find out why she didn't show up. He didn't call home to ask his mother if Amanda at least attempted to go out, because he didn't want to be hurt again.

She had already said that it was his fault that she was on Malatha. She said that she wanted to go home and see her grandmother. Aiden didn't want to fight anymore. He was tired. All he ever wanted was for Amanda to say she loved him and really mean it, but she could not do that.

He got out the car and walked up the drive to the front door and to his surprise, he heard music. It was his favorite song by The Stargazers. He pushed the door open, and there she was.

Amanda was standing right in front of him, holding his favorite dessert.

"Surprise!" she shouted. "I made your favorite molten pudding! Your mother said you love this dessert and that it was your favorite," Amanda said smiling.

He went up to her and hugged her.

"It is, thank you," Aiden said smiling.

He looked into Amanda's eyes and he could see the love for him written in her pupils.

"I'm sorry, Aiden. For the things I said to you the other day. I didn't mean them. I love you more than anything in this world and I choose to be with you."

"I thought I wanted to see my grandmother and brother again and go back to Earth, but I didn't know that I was surrounded by people who loved me right here on Malatha. But, I hope that one day I would see my grandmother and brother again. I pray to God that they are okay. I know it's not for me to go back to Earth, and that perhaps I am supposed to be here with you. God put us together. He brought you from across the galaxy to be with me. I love you. I want to spend my life with you," Amanda said as she looked into Aiden's eyes.

Aiden hugged her tight and his heart poured out of his chest. His eyes filled with tears because he had heard what he needed to hear from Amanda. He wanted her to choose him over her grandmother and Steve. He wanted her whole heart. Finally, she did choose him and gave him her whole heart.

His dreams had come true. He had a wife to share his life and start a family with. Maybe even have a son to carry on his family name. He picked Amanda up, swung her around, and kissed her. Amanda smiled happily.

She was happy that she chose to be with Aiden and now she could open her heart up to him and love him like he loved her.

She knew that her grandmother would want that and she will be happy for her. She was going to become the best wife she could be. Not only for Aiden, but for her grandmother and Steve. Maybe one day she would see them again.

Amanda and Aiden took the pudding into the kitchen. Amanda got a plate for Aiden so that she could give him some. Aiden sat down at the kitchen island and ate his pudding. Aaron and Abigail walked into the kitchen and Amanda got them plates as well.

"How did everything go at work, son?" Aaron asked.

"Everything went according to plan. We arrested Barnabas and the women are all going to receive infusement treatment."

Amanda's eyes widened because she was supposed to go and meet that man. She jumped when Aiden mentioned his name. Aiden looked at her.

"Don't worry. For all the women who didn't show up, they won't get into any trouble because they decided to change their minds and they didn't break any law."

"That's good, Aiden," Abigail said as she looked at Amanda.

"I was going to go and meet Barnabas last night, but I thought about how much I love you Aiden. And I couldn't make myself hurt you or your family. So, I stayed here. I hope you could forgive me," Amanda said looking at Aiden.

Aiden looked at her and his heart went out for her.

"I forgive you and I love you more than life itself."

CHAPTER

Barnabas and Cyr sat motionless in the courtroom as the judge read off their charges. They didn't have a defense, because Barnabas had decided to plead guilty. They sat and listened to the charges that the prosecutor had piled up against them and Barnabas began to feel numb. A little tension began to move down his spine.

He wanted to jump up and plead not guilty, but he thought of his brother Drogo and the kind of life he could have if he got a lighter sentence. So, he sat there stoned-faced and stared down the judge. The judge was angry and appalled. He hated that Barnabas tried to undermine everything that the government tried to do.

He looked at Barnabas and his stomach turned. All he wanted to do was sentence him to death.

"Barnabas Drapers and Cyr Star. You heard the charges that were brought against you. How do you plead?" the judge said angrily.

Barnabas looked at the judge with no remorse.

"Guilty," he said.

Cyr, on the other hand, was frightened and confused, but he had promised Barnabas that he was going to plead guilty. He looked at Barnabas and then at the judge and lowered his head.

"Guilty," he mumbled.

The audience in the courtroom was stunned and outraged. They began to shout at Barnabas and Cyr.

"Sociopath!"

The judge pounded on the bench with his mallet.

"Order in the court! Order in the court," he shouted.

But the crowd kept shouting. "Sociopath!"

Barnabas looked motionless at the crowd and said nothing.

Cyr lowered his head and began crying.

"Order in the court!" the judge shouted until the crowd calmed down and got quiet.

"Barnabas and Cyr, since your plea is guilty and you knew the consequences of breaking the law, I have no other choice but to sentence you to death by lethal injection until you are both dead!"

Barnabas looked motionless at the judge as he gave them their sentence while Cyr began to sob loudly.

The guards came and got Barnabas and Cyr and took them back to their cell.

"Can I talk to Colonel Galveston?" Barnabas asked the guard who was in charge.

"It's very important. I must see him."

"I'll let him know you want to see him, Barnabas," the guard said.

Col. Galveston was talking to the judge in the courtroom when the guard walked up to him and handed him a note. The note said Barnabas wanted to see him at once.

"Excuse me, judge. This is important," Col. Galveston said as he walked out of the courtroom.

He walked back to Barnabas' cell. Barnabas was pacing up and down his room.

"You wanted to see me, Barnabas?" Galveston asked.

"Yes, I did what you asked. I pleaded guilty. I know it's too late for me, but my brother, Drogo. Are you going to keep your word and give him a lighter sentence?" Barnabas asked.

Col. Galveston looked at Barnabas.

"Yes, I'm going to keep my word since Drogo had little to do with your plans. He will get a lighter sentence."

Barnabas was relieved that at least Drogo could be free.

"Thank you, Colonel," he said.

Col. Galveston looked at Barnabas but felt no remorse for him. He was glad that Barnabas was behind bars. He wanted to throw away the key, but Barnabas and Cyr were going to be executed. So, he walked away with a smile on his face.

"Barnabas, they caught us, and we are going down. But I'm glad it's you that I'm going down with. You have been my friend for over twenty years. My only friend," Cyr said sobbing and feeling a little nervous.

"Don't get soft on me now Cyr. We are going to go down like men. We did the crime, now we have to suffer the consequence. You knew the risk when you decided to go in with me. So, shape up," Barnabas said as he put his hand on Cyr's shoulder.

"My only regret is that I let Drogo down. That's why I pleaded guilty. So, he could have some kind of life. Drogo is a good boy. He doesn't deserve this."

"I'm the snake," Barnabas said as he stared out of the window.

"No, Drogo doesn't deserve this," Cyr cried.

Drogo was in his cell by himself. He wasn't scheduled to be executed. So, Galveston had little concern for him.

"Can I see my brother one last time before he goes," Drogo asked Galveston.

"I don't see why not. I'll arrange for a guard to take you to see him at one o'clock," Galveston said.

Drogo lay in his cell sobbing.

"I told Barnabas that we will get caught but he wouldn't listen. You think you know everything. Now you are going to die, and I'll be alone," Drogo cried as he kicked his feet onto the wall of the cell.

When it was time to see Barnabas, Drogo walked in the visitor's room and looked at Barnabas one last time. Barnabas looked at Drogo and his heart dropped. He didn't feel sorry for himself. He felt for Drogo, because he knew that Drogo was going to be alone.

"What am I going to do now?" Drogo asked.

"You are a man, Drogo. When you get out of here take my ship and go away."

"Make a life for yourself and don't look back. You have a chance to make something out of yourself. Don't be like me. Make mom proud of you," Barnabas said.

Drogo began to cry.

"Stop that! Don't you cry! You are a man! Men don't cry! Now go back to your cell and don't look back."

"I will Barnabas. I'm going to make something out of myself, brother."

CHAPTER
46

The Malatha citizens were stunned and outraged when they heard the news about Barnabas and his plans to take some women to Cyprus Five to sell them into sex slavery. They stormed down to the federal court building to protest and voice their opinion.

Col. Galveston made sure that every person on the planet of Malatha knew the consequences of harming their new women citizens. He made Barnabas' trial public in an attempt to frighten other criminals from doing the same or something worse.

The crowd outside the court building grew larger as the people protested and set fires. Everyone wanted to get a glimpse of Barnabas and Cyr. They listened as Barnabas gave his plea and when they heard guilty, they began to riot.

The police had to control the crowd with riot gear.

"How could he do this? My wife was one of those women he victimized!" a man shouted.

"How could they let this happen?! The government was supposed to protect those women! Now they let something like this happen!" he continued.

The crowd had gotten larger and they protested well over into the night. A few uncontrollable men had broken into stores and looted. The crowd had stopped traffic on Federal Drive, a large busy street that led to the business section of the city.

"We demand answers!" they shouted.

"How could this happen? The government let this happen!"

Prime Minister Raincourt had sent Col. Galveston out to talk to the crowd in an attempt to calm them down. Col. Galveston had ordered a special task force to control the crowd. When the task force got out onto the street, they began shooting in the crowd with their phasers which stung some of them.

The crowd dispersed in every direction and then began to go home. Galveston had set a curfew at eleven o'clock for every citizen of Surrok. He then had a press conference and every citizen of Malatha watched. They tried to get answers from the government. The press conference was set for 8:00 p.m. and everyone tuned in.

Col. Galveston walked up to the podium and looked into the camera.

"Citizens of Malatha. I know that you are outraged at what had happened with Barnabas Drapers and Cyr Star. I assure you that we won't let anything like this happen ever again."

"When we informed you that we were bringing women here to live among us, we explained to you the laws we put forth to protect those women. We told you the consequences of breaking those laws. Barnabas and Cyr broke those laws and they will be dealt with the harshest of punishment, while the women who tried to go with them will be dealt with accordingly."

"So, I urge each and every one of you to stay home and let the authorities handle this under the law. And I warn anyone else who plans to do something like this. They will be caught and dealt with just as severely as Barnabas and Cyr. So, get off the street and let us deal with Barnabas and Cyr."

"They will be getting the maximum sentence for their crime," Galveston said.

The people of Malatha watched the press conference, but they were still outraged. They began to gather in secret and others like Dr. Ingram LeBlanc had called a meeting of his own. He was outraged about the treatment toward his wife, Hope.

So, he gathered together as many men as he could whose wives received infusement treatment. He wanted to plan a protest of his own and march down Federal Drive.

"Look men, my wife and your wives were treated unfairly! Are they not citizens?! How could they get a sentence without a trial or jury? I thought my wife was equal to me! How could they do this to us? Now, my wife is sick and confused! She was perfectly healthy before she got infusement treatment!"

"That treatment is for violent criminals! My wife was no criminal! So, I want answers!" he told the men as he tried to rouse them up.

The men yelled as they gather around, "We want answers! We want answers!"

"Well, come on! Let's march down Federal Drive and demand answers!" LeBlanc yelled as he got his protest sign and began marching down the street in front of the courthouse.

"What about our wives?!"

"We want justice for our wives!"

"We want justice for our wives!"

CHAPTER

Amanda was ashamed that she had talked to Barnabas and was considering going with him. She was embarassed because she knew that Aiden and his parents knew what she was attempting to do.

She wanted to run away and hide. She felt so bad she stayed in her room all day. Abigail came to her door and asked her if she wanted to eat lunch with her, but Amanda pretended to be asleep. She felt so bad that her body began to ache.

"Why me?" she thought.

"Why do bad things always happen to me?" she said as she pulled the covers over her head.

"Well, it's not all bad, at least I didn't go. I changed my mind. That should count for something."

Then she thought of the other women, especially her friend Donna.

"My god! Donna, she got caught! She got infusement treatment! I have to go see her. Poor Milo! He didn't deserve that either. He is such a nice guy."

Amanda got up, ran into the bathroom, turned on the shower, and stepped in. She washed all over and tried to rinse away her guilt. When she got dressed, she went downstairs to the family room. It was almost time for Barnabas' trial to come on the viewing screen.

Amanda sat on the couch and exhaled. Her stomach was in knots.

"How could he do this? He had all of us fooled," she thought.

The trial came on the viewing screen and Amanda watched as Barnabas had no remorse for what he tried to do. Her stomach turned to knots and her legs began to shake. She wanted to cry when she heard what his plans were.

"How could you?!" she screamed.

Abigail walked into the family room and sat on the couch.

"I can't believe that Barnabas would stoop so low. When we talked, he was convincing and charming. I really thought that he was going to take us back to Earth. I never thought he was lying," Amanda said with tears in her eyes.

"I'm so ashamed," she said to Abigail.

"Don't be ashamed. It could have happened to anyone. Besides, you changed your mind. You didn't go. That's what matters now."

"Barnabas? That's how criminals are. They could be cunning. He is a vicious liar who didn't care how many people he hurt as long as he got what he wanted," Abigail said.

Amanda felt a little better, but her stomach was still in knots. She wanted to somehow make it up to Aiden.

They watched the trial on the viewing screen. Amanda was surprised at the reaction of the Malatha citizens.

"It looks like it's going to be a riot downtown," she said as she watched the protesters.

"I hope Aiden is all right. He is at the courthouse," Abigail said.

Aiden had come home early after the trial. He had told Abigail and Amanda everything that went on at the courthouse. Abigail was relieved that Aiden made it home safely.

"After dinner, could you take me to go see Donna and Milo?" Amanda asked.

"Yes, I wanted to go see them myself. I want to let Milo know he has my support."

"I'm sorry Aiden, for everything that happened. I was stupid and selfish and I didn't think of anyone but myself. Now, look at what happened. I should have told you what Barnabas was planning from the beginning," Amanda said to Aiden with tears in her eyes.

"I know you are sorry, Amanda. Come on now, stop crying. Don't worry about it. You are safe here with me. That's all that matters. I know now that you love me and I'm not going to take that for granted. We are a team now and I won't let anyone or anything break us up. Not Barnabas or De Ivory or anyone. So, don't worry anymore. It's all behind us now," Aiden said smiling as he wiped Amanda tears.

"After dinner, we will go visit Donna and see how she is coming along," he said.

"Thank you, Aiden, for not giving up on me. Thank you for loving me," Amanda said with joy in her heart.

"You're welcome," Aiden said as he kissed her on the forehead.

Abigail came into the room and turned off the viewing screen.

"Ah, that man, he gives me the creeps. Aiden, were you there when he pleaded guilty?" she asked Aiden.

"Yes, and he had no remorse. It was like he didn't care that he was going to get executed. You know he got a plea deal for his brother Drogo."

"He's getting off easy," Abigail looked at Aiden.

"What? Is he?" Amanda looked at Aiden and her jaw dropped.

"He was just as guilty!" she yelled.

"I know, calm down," Aiden said.

"Col. Galveston let him get off because he's only twenty-four, and they only want Barnabas and Cyr." Amanda looked at Aiden.

"I don't get it. He is just as guilty. What message does that give to other criminals? You can get off a crime because you are young?" Amanda asked angrily.

Aiden looked at her.

"Don't worry, Amanda. It's all over now. Barnabas was the leader and he is being executed. So, justice is being served."

"Well, I'm tired of hearing about it. Let's go eat dinner and put all of this behind us," Abigail said as she looked at Aiden. "I cooked your favorite stew. So, come on. Let's go eat before it gets cold."

"Yeah, I'm starving," Amanda said, forcing a smile as she thought about Barnabas.

No matter how hard she tried, she couldn't get Barnabas out of her mind. She just couldn't understand how he could do what he had done. Now she had to think about Drogo getting off. She knew that he probably didn't think of the idea of taking the women to Cyprus Five, but he should have gotten at least a harsher punishment than what he was going to receive.

CHAPTER

Dr. Ingram LeBlanc and other husbands of the women who were caught with Barnabas staged a protest outside Prime Minister Raincourt's office. Dr. Ingram LeBlanc stood up to the podium and shouted out.

"Our women were wronged! Raincourt and the other cabinet members gave our wives infusement treatment without a trial or a sentence! Aren't our wives equal citizens of Malatha or are they properties of the government to be dealt with as the Prime Minister sees fit?"

"I thought my wife Hope was an equal partner to me. A human being, with all the rights and protection of any other citizen under the law of Malatha, but the government said otherwise. The government said that they would be dealt with as the government sees fit!"

"My wife Hope didn't even have a chance to defend herself!" LeBlanc shouted as the crowd grew larger and angry.

"Is it fair?! Could the government give our wives infusement treatment without an explanation?" LeBlanc shouted.

"Yeah!" the men shouted.

"We want justice for our wives!"

"We want justice for our wives!"

The men shouted, holding up pictures of the women who received infusement treatment.

"We want justice for our wives!" shouted the men.

The police came to try to control the crowd, but the crowd had begun to grow larger and out of control. They took their protest to the streets and marched down to the business district to prevent shoppers from shopping.

Prime Minister Raincourt and the cabinet members were in the conference room, looking out the window at the protesters. Prime Minister Raincourt turned on the news on the viewing screen.

"Over ten thousand protesters are marching down federal court to the business district. They plan to stage a sit in to block shoppers from shopping. They plan to cripple businesses and stop traffic on the busy Federal Drive where people come to shop and conduct business. They will continue to do this until they get some answers," the reporter said.

"Oh, no. This is bad! Election day is coming up! I have to get on this quick!" Raincourt said to De Ivory.

"Maybe we can wait. After all, the men knew the laws when they took home a wife. It was in the contract," De Ivory said.

"Besides those women broke the law. They tried to escape. If they would have been successful, the men would be outraged at that," Galveston said.

"What we really have to look at is whether or not our new women citizens have equal rights under our laws or are they second-class citizens?" Raincourt asked.

"Well, we wanted them to be equals with all rights and privileges of our male citizens. I still think our laws are fair, but we should have charged them under the law and gave them a fair trial with a jury of their peers. So, because of that, we were wrong," De Ivory said.

"Okay. Because they were punished without a trial or jury, we will compensate them," Raincourt said.

Prime Minister Raincourt and the other cabinet members had called a press conference. Raincourt stood up to the podium.

"Citizens of Malatha, these are troubling times."

"We have welcomed new female citizens to our planet and because of this, we found ourselves in a position that is new to us and with problems that we did not have to deal with before. We heard you asking, 'Are these new citizens equal citizens under the law of Malatha?'"

"And the answer is yes."

"Under our human rights laws, they are equal as you and I, but there are some laws that the new citizens are not so equal. And we talked about that in the beginning, when we brought them here."

"Should the women have had a fair trial under the law of Malatha before they were punished?"

"My answer to that is yes!"

"They should have had a fair trial and because of that, I have decided to compensate each and every family who was injured because of this scandal. Having new female citizens here in Malatha is new to us! We are still trying to write the laws so that they could be fair to everyone."

"Are we going to get it right the first time? My answer to this is no."

"But we are going to learn from our mistakes and move on because we are a resilient race with laws that are fair and right for everyone!"

Prime Minister Raincourt stated before he ended the press conference.

Dr. Ingram LeBlanc and the other protesters watched the press conference on the viewing screen. They cheered when they heard that they would be compensated. After Raincourt ended the press conference, the crowd began to go home.

LeBlanc felt proud he had gotten victory for Hope who was recovering at the treatment center. He couldn't wait to tell her that the protest was a success. The other men ran to the center to tell their wives.

"All I wanted was justice for Hope," LeBlanc said to a reporter.

"She didn't deserve this. That Barnabas tricked her and told her that he was going to take her home. I understand why she did it. Under the circumstances of her being here, I would want to go home too. So, we got justice for our wives!" LeBlanc shouted as he walked away.

Prime Minister Raincourt was relieved that the Drapers Scandal was behind them and that things were finally going back to normal. The women were recovering from the treatment well and Raincourt had decided to use infusement treatment only as a last resort.

"From now on, when our new women citizens commit a crime, they will be treated like the male citizens of Malatha and be given a trial with the jury of their peers. And their punishment will fit their crime," Prime Minister Raincourt said to the cabinet members and to the women who were appointed Ambassadors of the Earth Women.

CHAPTER

Donna was recovering well from the infusement treatment. Some days were worse than others. Some of her symptoms were nausea and headaches, but she felt that she couldn't get past the vomiting.

Her speech was still slurred and on many occasions, she had double vision. But as the days went by, she got stronger and stronger.

Chancellor De Ivory and the therapist worked with Donna to help her with her speech and balance. It was hard for her to walk at first, but now she can stand and move slowly down the hall alone. Donna's will was strong. She kept telling herself that she was going to beat this and that she was going to be better than she was before.

So she worked with the speech therapist and practiced saying the words on her flashcards every day. She also exercised and took walks in the hall. De Ivory was impressed with her progress. She was recovering far faster than the other women. They were doing well also, but not as well as Donna.

Donna felt bad about the whole thing. She wanted to get better for Milo's sake. He didn't deserve to have a cripple for a wife. Milo was there at the infusement treatment center with Donna every day when she was there. He wouldn't let her go through the treatment alone.

He had decided to stay with Donna and try to make their marriage work. He had helped Donna practice her speech by showing her flashcards. And he walked with her along the hall. He was happy that Donna was improving in ways that showed little signs of the treatment.

He had sat down and talked to Chancellor De Ivory, and discussed his and Donna's future together. He wanted to know if Donna could still have a family. De Ivory reassured him that she could. He told him to give her a year and she will be ready to physically and mentally have and raise children.

He also talked to Col. Galveston and asked him for a furlough so he could take Donna to the mountains. He felt that being in nature would also help her recover. Donna tried to apologize on many occasions to Milo.

But Milo told her that he understood why she tried to run away and he didn't have any ill will against her. That made Donna feel a little bit better about things. Aiden took Amanda to the center to see Donna and Milo. They were relieved that the infusement treatment did little damage.

Donna was in good spirits. She was glad to see Amanda. Amanda felt bad that Donna got caught and that she changed her mind and didn't show up. She had apologized to Donna and told her everything that had happened.

Donna smiled. "I'm glad that you didn't show up."

"I wouldn't wish infusement treatment on anyone," she said.

"Holly, Grace, and I are going to take some classes together at the Civics Center," Amanda said.

"I promise when I get better, I'm going to join you," Donna said.

Donna laughed and talked just like old times. Amanda couldn't tell that she was sick. That made Amanda feel better. She walked with Donna in the hall. They walked down to the big window and looked out the garden.

"I'm glad I could enjoy seeing a beautiful garden again. I took it for granted before, but now every day that I'm alive, I'm grateful," Donna said with tears in her eyes.

Amanda looked at her.

"Me too," she said.

Milo was happy that he still had friends who cared.

"Thank you guys for coming. I couldn't do this without your support," Milo said to Aiden.

Aiden looked at Milo. He knew Milo ever since they were cadets in the military academy. They were inseparable. Bartholomew, Basil, and Milo were like brothers. They did everything together.

Now Milo needed his help and he was going to do everything in his power to help him.

"You are welcome, Milo. If you or Donna need anything, I'm a phone call away," Aiden said. "Do you think Donna is improving?" "She is getting stronger every day," Milo reassured.

"Yes, it seems as if she never got the treatment," Aiden commented.

"I can't wait to take her to the mountains. I know she would love it out there. My father used to take me when I was young. Now, I get to take her and someday I'm going to take our son," Milo said.

"Yeah, maybe we can take our sons together," Aiden said.

"Remember when they first told us that they were going to bring the women here to live among us?" Aiden asked Milo. "Remember when we used to talk about how our wives would look and how they would be? We made a pact that our children would know one another and grow up together."

"And we would be neighbors and go on vacations together. Yeah, I remember," Milo said.

"It's funny. Now, those days are here. We can do just that," Aiden said.

"Our sons can grow up together and go to the Academy. I hope that Donna would be all right and that she would be able to have a son."

"I pray every night for her. De Ivory said she would be able to. He told me not to worry," Milo said with tears in his eyes.

Aiden looked at him and his heart went out for him.

"Don't worry, brother. Donna is getting better day by day. One day you and Donna would have a house full of children," Aiden said as he put his hand on Milo's shoulder.

Milo looked at him and wiped his eyes.

"I hope so man."

Donna and Amanda came into the room.

"Well, brother. We better be going. I have to be at work early tomorrow." Amanda hugged Donna and then she hugged Milo.

"Take care you two," she said.

"Donna, you really look great," she continued.

"Thank you, Amanda," Donna said smiling.

Aiden shook Milo's hand.

"I'll see you tomorrow, brother," he said as they walked out of the door.

CHAPTER 50

Chancellor De Ivory had brought Estelle Cook with him to his office. She was a tall, medium-complexioned black woman with long black braids. He had brought the wedding contract up on the computer screen.

"You see Estelle, just as I promised before the Barnabas scandal, we will be husband and wife. All I have to do is sign the contract. That's all to it," he said to Estelle smiling.

Estelle smiled and her heart skipped a beat. She waited almost a year for a match.

Now she was going to be Mrs. De Ivory.

"I'm glad, Wendell. I've waited a long time for this day."

"I've waited a long time for you," De Ivory said as he looked at Estelle, and his face blushed.

"Well, you don't have to wait much longer."

"I'm sorry I kept you at the compound, but I wanted you to be near me until I was able to choose you," De Ivory said as he signed the contract.

"There, I signed it. We are husband and wife," he said as he picked her up and swung her around. Estelle hugged him and they kissed.

"You are going to love our house. It's large enough for a big family. I have a large backyard with lots of flowers and plants."

"I think you will love my neighborhood. It's nice too. It has a large park, and lots of shops and stores. And until you learn to drive, we are close to public transportation. I was thinking we should have a party and invite all of my friends and colleagues so they could get acquainted with you. But we want to do that until after you give our house a bit of a woman's touch. I really only live in one room," De Ivory said smiling.

Estelle looked at him and smiled back.

"I know how men are. It takes a woman to make a house a home," she said smiling.

"We would have to go shopping so I could cook a big dinner for you. I know just what I want to cook. I was reading a recipe at the compound, but first, we have to get the ingredients."

"Oh, yeah? And what is this you want to cook?" De Ivory asked.

"Curry Tolapie Stew," Estelle said smiling.

De Ivory's jaw dropped.

"Are you sure you want to cook that? That's not an easy dish to make. It takes a lot of preparation."

"I know, but I'm up for the challenge," Estelle said smiling.

Col. Galveston knocked on De Ivory's door.

The chancellor looked up.

"I wonder who could that be?" he said to Estelle.

Estelle walked over to the couch and sat down.

De Ivory sat on his desk.

"Come in," he said.

Col. Galveston came into the office.

"Chancellor, I heard you brought Estelle here today. Did you sign the contract?" he asked smiling.

De Ivory smiled.

"I did. Estelle, this is Col. Galveston. You may know him from the ship."

Estelle smiled. "I remember. How do you do, Colonel?" she said as she reached out her hand so he could shake it.

"I'm fine, Estelle. It is nice to finally meet you," Col. Galveston said as he shook her hand.

"Chancellor, we should go out to dinner soon. You and Estelle, and Chantel and I. It will be fun," Col. Galveston said.

"Yes, it would be nice," De Ivory said.

"I have a bit of a good news. Chantel is pregnant!" the colonel said excitedly.

De Ivory's eyes widened and he clapped his hands together.

"That is good news! Congratulations! I'm happy for you."

"I'm happy. I'm a bit nervous, though. I don't know if it is going to be a boy or a girl, but I'm hoping for a boy. I guess I want my son to go to the Academy like I did. I want him to be athletic too. I want to take him to Dacia, show him Mount Tanja and how magical it is."

"I remember the time when my father first took me. He showed me the Golden Circle and my eyes lit up. I've never seen anything so beautiful. We camped out there for a whole week. My father told me that I should take my son one day to keep the tradition alive, but because we had a shortage of women, I thought I would never be able to have a son. I thought our race was dying until we brought the Earth women here. Now my wife is pregnant, and I have a fifty-fifty chance of having a boy," Galveston said to De Ivory.

De Ivory looked at him. "Well if you have a girl, you can still take her to Mount Tanja and show her the Golden Circle. She will be just as pleased. She could even go to the Academy. There are so many things a girl can do just as well."

"I know. I didn't mean that. I just wanted a boy. A girl would be just as nice. I don't care if it's a boy or girl. I don't care. All I know is I'm going to be a father," Galveston said smiling.

"That's great. I'm happy for you too," Estelle said.

"So, what do you two plan for tonight?" Galveston asked.

"Well, Estelle wants to make Curry Tolapie Stew. I was going to help her and show her my kitchen, but first, we have to go shopping."

"That sounds like a lot of fun. Well, I have to go home. Chantel cooked dinner for me tonight as well. I swear I put on ten pounds since I got married. I think I'm going to have to join a gym," Col. Galveston said laughing.

"Well, we are going to have to be partners at the gym if Estelle keeps getting ideas about recipes," De Ivory said laughing.

CHAPTER

Aiden was in good spirits on his way home from work. Barnabas' trail was behind him. All the women who had received infusement treatment were in recovery and Amanda was safe and sound at home. He stopped at a dress shop at the shopping center on his way home. He saw a beautiful long white lace dress. That reminded him of the dress his mother got married in thirty years earlier.

He imagined Amanda wearing the dress as she walked along the beach to get married to him in a traditional Malatha wedding. His heart fluttered when he thought how pretty Amanda would be in that dress. He parked his car and went into the dress shop.

"How may I help you?" asked the shop clerk. She was a tall, olive-skinned woman wearing a long black dress with yellow and pink flowers in it.

"I would like to take a closer look at that dress hanging by the window?" Aiden asked smiling.

"Ah, the white lace dress?" the clerk asked.

"Yes," Aiden said.

She went over and got the dress. She gave it to Aiden.

"This is a very special dress. It came from Dacia. It is a traditional Dacia wedding gown. It was handcrafted from the finest material," The clerk said.

"I would like to buy it for my wife," Aiden said.

"She must be special?" the clerk said as she looked at Aiden.

Aiden smiled. "She is."

The woman put the dress in a garment bag.

"We have shoes and a veil to match," she said.

"I'll take that too," Aiden said.

The woman got the shoes and veil and put them in a separate box. Aiden put his thumbprint on a purchase pad and the purchase went into his account. He got his items and headed for his car. It was early evening and the sun was just going down behind the ocean.

Aiden liked sunsets; it somehow calmed him. He thought about everything that happened and he thanked God that Amanda was safe with his parents at home. He wanted to do something special for Amanda. He wanted to make their marriage as normal as possible.

Aiden drove slowly home. The air was warm on his face and the sudden breeze made Aiden's heart dance. He was in better spirits than he was when he left work. He couldn't wait to see the look on Amanda's face when she sees the dress he had just bought. He thought that he would propose to Amanda and have a traditional Malatha wedding, along with a cake and a band playing traditional Malatha music. Amanda would love that. She always wanted a wedding.

He thought that he would invite all of his friends and relatives. Then afterward, they would take a cruise around Malatha, Aiden thought as he was pleased with himself. He parked the car and walked slowly up to the house.

He walked into the house and Abigail and Amanda were in the kitchen preparing dinner. Aiden walked into the kitchen and hugged Amanda.

"Hi baby," he said as he kissed her.

Amanda smiled and shivered all over as she kissed Aiden back.

"How was your day?" Amanda asked as she turned and finished setting the table.

"It was fine. Everything's back to normal since Barnabas is gone. Chancellor De Ivory took a vacation. He chose a wife on Monday. Col. Galveston said I could take a couple of days off," Aiden said smiling.

"I thought we might go to the mountains for the weekend," he said. "I thought we might fly. You have never gone flying. You will love it. It will be fun," Aiden said to Amanda.

"That sounds great!" Amanda said excitedly.

Aaron walked into the kitchen.

"What's taken so long?" he asked. "I'm starving."

"I was just about to call you. Dinner's ready," Abigail said.

They sat down and Aiden looked at Amanda. He placed his hand on hers.

"Amanda," he said looking into her eyes.

"I know I was the one who chose you and you didn't have a say in the matter, but I loved you from the first day I saw you and I wanted you to be my wife. You make me happy every minute we are together and I promise you I would do everything in my power to make you happy and safe."

"I know that on Earth, the women have a nice church wedding with a pretty gown, flowers, and horses. Afterward, they have a reception," Aiden said as he got down on his knee.

He held Amanda's hand and looked her in the eyes.

"Amanda, would you do me the honor of being my wife?"

Amanda's heart jumped in her chest and tears filled her eyes.

"Yes," she said, pressing back the emotion that was boiling up inside of her.

"I would be honored to be your wife and I would try with all of my heart to make you happy," Amanda said.

Aiden smiled and kissed Amanda. Abigail and Aaron smiled as they watch their son propose to his first love. Abigail wiped the tears from her eyes. Aaron grabbed Abigail by the hand and squeezed it. Aiden smiled as he looked at Amanda. His heart jolted because he knew that he had found the one. He had found love, like what his father had with his mother. Amanda would always and forever be at his side.

After all of these years, his dream had finally come true and he knew that he could trust Amanda with all of his heart. He loved her from the first time he saw her on the ship and he knew in his heart that Amanda was the one for him. For as long as Amanda lived, he will be there right by her side.

Printed by Libri Plureos GmbH in Hamburg, Germany